THE UNHOLY ONES

MARTIN BERRY

ISBN 978-1-953223-52-4 (paperback)
ISBN 978-1-953223-51-7 (hardcover)
ISBN 978-1-953223-50-0 (digital)

Rushmore Press LLC
1 800 460 9188
www.rushmorepress.com

Printed in the United States of America

CHAPTER I

Darkness fell on the city around ten o'clock each night. This is the summer of 2019 with the bikers making their arrival no secret. Roaring engines, screams of delight and just to be a nuisance for the town was their passion. The UnHoly Ones Came to town with trouble around every fucking corner.

The cops knew this yet one in particular Sgt Ray Blue had the experience with these outlaws twice before. He was getting used to the manner in which they conducted themselves, with little or no regard for the town but were mainly interested in the young ladies of this fair city.

"Hello Sarge, how are you tonight?" asked Constable Wicker. Finding the small man behind one of four desks in the office Ray had to take a second look before he asked,

"Excuse me. Do I know you?" There had been a change of new recruits set out by law # 346 where the Government could and would place new men into areas where it was peaceful to give them a feel of being a cop before they were sent to areas mostly needed.

"Gee Sarge don't you remember the riots of 2017 where I introduced myself when you were speaking to the Mayor about prison reform?"

wicker was a small man with beady eyes wearing bi-focals to enhance his vision. Ray scratched his head trying to conger in his mind the meet but for the life of him he could not.

"I can't recollect right now but if it did happen then it will come to me. What's your name?"

"Its Wicker sir. John Wicker." Ray nodded at him then turning to his right walked into his own office. Sitting behind his desk in a lazy like chair Ray pondered on the tale told by his constable. It had been a terrible time for the city of Salem with all the civil rights riots against east Indians taking jobs from Americans who put not only their energy but also their lives into holding jobs to make the government t work. It was a terrible scene for the true blue americans but Ray had to follow orders even though he did not agree with the decisions of the federal government, but that was politics of the stupid bureaucrats that ran the country or thought they did. Going back out to the inner office he came up to the constable's desk as he had a small recollection of meeting the man.

"It seems to come back to me about meeting you. You say you're name is Wicker right?"

The small constable nodded yes.

"How is it you being a seasoned officer now sits behind a desk?" Ray asked confused.

"I got in some shit last year so they decided than just axing me they would send me out here. I'm lucky to still be with the Police force." Ray began remembering something terrible that besmirched the fine name of the Police so he carried on his questioning.

"Were you involved in that rash of break and enters? They found, what, five officers on the take?

"Yeah sarge they did." He admitted with his head low. Going on he related what his part was in he crimes the cops committed.

"I didn't know what they were doing at the time. I found a young cop going through a stereo shop and I kept it quiet. When he got busted, he rolled over on me and so here I am. They sent me out here for some rehabilitation."

Ray looked him straight in the eyes telling him something already on his mind.

"You can count your blessing because if I were the Chief I would have gotten rid of the whole lot of you so you wouldn't be here at all." As he caught his breath he continued on for he had a lot to say.

"It looks good on you Wicker. I have no sympathy whatsoever for dirty cops. You may have not stole anything but you were counted as one of them for keeping quiet when a felony was going on. You are just as dirty as they were." Wicker got his dander up as he stood to tell his Sargeant off, questioning him.

"Who the hell nominated you God? I stuck up for a fellow officer and I get shit upon by all departments. You have no sympathy for cops who take care of one another do you? Well the way the courts are handing out sentences we are fighting a losing battle. Why not enjoy life a little better? The badge does not stand for the same things anymore, not now, no, not ever again."

Ray could not believe his ears hearing this horseshit from a fellow officer. Ray was a cop's cop. He hated it when these lousy cops, who would take a pay-off were ready to pass the blame on the courts or even their own partners so they would be gratified from blame. They could not understand why accusations from the Chief came their way but if it did and it did, who wants to go down alone? Sgt Ray Blue was always thinking. Never would he allow his mind to rest especially when a criminal factor came into play because it was a force of evil to him, anyways the cops were supposed to be the good guys.

CHAPTER II

Twelve-thirty-five. Outside an all night convenience store, the boys in blue had a robber staked out. Trying to reason with him was out of the question as he wanted certain guarantees which was not going to happen. The robber was a young black guy who was scared shitless as he watched through the window the cops squatting behind their squad cars waiting for the opportunity to fire at him. Not knowing what to do he listened as the cops, using a blow horn called out to him. His mind was racing as he looked at the hostages he had. He came into the convenience shop several times figuring it would be a good place for some fast cash to support his crystal meth addiction. He was wrong. Being a member of the UnHoly Ones, a renegade bike group he figured it would be a piece of cake. Then things changed as Sgt Ray Blue came to the scene.

"Okay fuckhead. Come on out now. Its twelve-thirty-five, at twelve-thirty-seven you run out of options." Sgt ray Blue hated these guys who rode bikes across America thinking they could do whatever they pleased no matter what trouble they caused or whoever got hurt. The young man did come out at twelve-forty-five. Raising his hands above his head the idiot still holding the .357 Ray called out to him as he took out his .44 magnum pointing it straight at the robber letting him know his intentions.

"ok fuckhead one more warning, drop the gun or die." The robber had a hold of a young girl with his other hand using her as bait to try to get out of this situation but he realized he had no chance at all so he figured he do a trick he used to do when he was a kid by tossing the gun to the ground and as it hit the ground it went off which startled some of the cops but not Sgt Ray Blue who had his gun levelled at the biker. It was a terrible scene as Sgt Ray Blue fired three shots at the robber killing him before he hit the ground. This encouraged the other cops to fire as well taking the life of the young girl being held as a hostage. It was just a terrible mess. This kid used to toss a gun on the ground making it go off scaring his friends, it was always a way of making him look supreme but today it cost him his life and also the young girl who he held hostage. Sgt Ray Blue had to call out to his fellow officers to stop shooting.

"Stop firing!" He yelled as a couple of more shots rang out. " Enough!" Silence filled the air as the cops straightened up to a standing position looking at the dead bodies in front of them. Sgt Ray Blue took a deep breath before proceeding over to where the bodies lay in a pool of blood. He knew there would terrible reprecussions for this terrible mess not only from Internal Affairs but also the Unholy Ones since one of their members was taken down by the Police. Calling Detective Davis who was the lead investigator for Internal Affairs, on the two way, Ray let him know the gist of what took place making sure he put it in a way that his officers would not get into trouble for the killing of the young girl.

Nothing much was said over the radio as it had too many ears. No Detective Davis would wait until he saw the report before finding out what really happened. After the meat wagon came to take the bodies away, Ray stayed a few more hours to answer any questions to his superiors. Then when it looked like it was over Ray headed for home. He was tired from what transpired throughout the whole day. Working for fourteen hours straight wore his nerves down so as soon as he got home he walked into the bathroom to fill the tub with hot water. Once he had it at the right temperature he left the bathroom going into the kitchen, opening the refrigerator he pulled a Bud. Cracking it open he headed back for the bathroom where he stripped down then climbed into the hot water to lay back, have his beer and try to relax. He knew Internal Affairs would all over him in the morning, not because of the dead biker but the innocent young girl who was snuffed out by an over eager cop. Someone had to answer for it.

After a couple of hours of just soaking in the wet warmth, Ray decided to finally get out. A hot bath always helped him to relax, to a certain extent anyways. Now going back into the kitchen he opened the refrigerator again to see what he had to eat. There was a bowl of left-overs from two days ago. Taking out the bowl he put it close to his nose to smell it hoping it was still good. It was tuna, chopped celery, green peppers, onions, salt & pepper and a healthy helping of mayo. He usually made a full bowl of it so he could use it in sandwiches to take to work. He had about enough for two sandwiches so getting out the bread he began making himself his supper. Going into the living-room he realized he was walking around nude, so thought it would be best if he had some clothes on incase someone came to his door. Then returning back to the living-room he plunked down in the lazyboy chair then let the television steal his thoughts for the evening. Nothing was on he really liked so he turned it over to the news catching a little about what had taken place earlier in town. Ray was not interested in listening to it from some reporter's point of view so he turned the television off just sitting where he was in the living-room. It was nearly three in the morning when Ray woke up still sitting in the lazyboy chair but he had a chill from the cool air of thee early morning. Getting up Ray went straight to his bedroom to sleep three more hours before he got up for the day. Pulling the blankets back, Ray crawled into the comfortable bed pulling the blankets up to his neck before dozing off again. Off went the alarm clock to let him k now it was time to get out of bed. Ray still had a chill on his arms so decided to have a hot shower which helped him tremendously. Waking up. Ray got out dried off and got partially dressed with his pants. He pulled on a white tee shirt to wear under his uniform shirt as it helped capture any sweat from the heat of the sun. Making himself a coffee he drank it black as usual to give him the needed oomph for the day so getting completely dressed as he sipped away on his coffee Ray was ready for work. Going outside he turned to face the door to lock it then get on his way.

Who was sitting waiting in Ray's office but Detective Davis. He had quite a few questions for the Sargeant as witnesses told Internal Affairs the young girl killed was done by a cop not the biker and that the biker had thrown the gun he carried on the ground where it accidentally went off which got the cops shooting killing him instantly but also a soft spoken sixteen year old girl.

Opening the door to his office he noticed the Detective making himself comfortable in the office so Ray did not hold back he walked straight in wanting to get this mess done and over with.

"Good Morning Ray." The Detective started.

"Good Morning." Ray answered.

"I have a few questions I need answers to get this finalized." The Detective offered as Ray took his seat behind his desk. Staring at the Detective Ray waited for a question, he wasn't going to give any indication of wrongdoing.

"Now Ray I took the opportunity to go out to the spot where this crime happened. Some of the townsfolk came forward giving statements which conflict with the report you wrote. I know things get carried away in situations like this but as a peace officer you have to hold the reins, sort of speak. I need the truth, that is what I am after here. Now in your statement you mention th3e biker was given an opportunity to surrender then when he came out he had his hand holding the weapon but it was raised as he had his arms in the air but with the other hand he held the young girl."

"Yes that is correct." Ray admitted as the Detective went on.

"When he threw the gun he was holding on the ground did that not tell you he was no longer a threat?"

"Yes this is true but when he did throw it to the ground somehow the gun went off and my fellow officers who are not as seasoned as I would like retuned fire killing the biker and with sadness the young girl."

"Well Sargeant I want the names of the officers you think are responsible for the shooting of the young girl." He stated as he looked Ray in the eyes showing he was not about to flinch. Ray was not about to flinch either. He got up from behind his desk to the door to lock it and then lower the blinds covering his office window. He did not want anyone to see or hear what transpired in the next hour or so.

"I don't know who you were talking to but my report is what had happened. Bring your witnesses in here and let's get to the bottom of the truth."

"Well from what I took down in statements there could have been a better way of handling the situation."

"What was I supposed to do? Let that fucking animal take down a couple of my officers. It was handled properly from my stand point as it was over in ten seconds if that. Now if someone has something else to mention then please bring him forward so we can hear his or her great advice on what had transpired. Haven't you got enough letters sent out to grieving families of officers lost in these stupid altercations? This was a threat not only to my officers but the general public. We cannot afford to allow trash like this to govern how the law works. We did what we had to do to settle the situation. Now if you have a problem with this then let me know right now." Ray was getting hot under the collar having to defend not only his officers but himself as well." Ray unlocked the door walking out of the office. He was tired, yes tired from all the bullshit that came with the job. It was now Ray was thinking strongly of packing it all in as a cop and venturing on his own as a Bounty Hunter of Private Eye. There certainly was money in it, a lot more than what he was making now. He thought of shoving his badge right up the Detective's ass. Thinking about it sort of broke the tension as Ray began to snicker then silently laugh at the thought of really taking his badge and shoving it up the Detective's ass. Wouldn't that be a pretty sight? The Captain's ass as well. The Captain was always looking over Ray's shoulder. It was a different kind of war now on the streets. Being a cop was once a trade many people wanted to be but nowadays it is no longer a favorite choice. No people now would rather be pimps or pushers.

CHAPTER III

It was Thursday night and ray wanted to be at home where he could relax from all the grief. He wanted to be with the only one who was his favorite. She had been his girl from high school, She had became his wife making him the most happiest man on the planet. She always had the right words to speak when he was overburdened with the job. Always smiling, not letting anything harm her disposition, ready to make sure everything was running smoothly for everyone. Ray remembered how she used to meet him at the door scantily clad showering him with love but most of she had something he needed most, a listening ear. Today was no different she would be back home from visiting her mother in Denver. As Ray parked in his driveway he walked into the house to be greeted by a delightful smile as she gently asked, " how was your day babe?" ray looked at her telling her.

"Well if getting blasted by the Captain and the head detective of Internal Affairs for putting a parasite in the ground is a normal day then yeah, I had a normal day."

Ray and his wife Claire had a seventeen month old baby boy to contend with which please Ray as he found solace in being with his boy. Ray was also deeply in love with his wife and this was evident when they walked down the streets of town, strange men would whistle at her, he would get so jealous that he swore he would go after those secret admirers but he had no reason to feel insecure. Claire loved him and only him. If anything happened to her man Claire had already decided she would stay single the rest of her days. So glad to have her back home he took her out to dinner so they could spend some time together which he needed to change the direction of his mind. Ray took her out away from the phones, away from anyone who might have an inkling to disrupt the time they had together. Tonight he even left his cell phone on the kitchen counter to make nothing interfered with either one of them. Going to Marnie's was one of Clair's favorite restaurants. It was a small quaint restaurant with good food and a live band each Saturday night. Tonight it was Friday so it meant they would pay attention to each other.

Back at the office the Police station was searching for Ray. They tried his phone several times getting a recording. Fear ran through some of the officers as a threat had been made against Ray. The Captain was worried about the bikers getting a hold of Ray and his family as they were now holding Ray responsible for the killing of their friend, their compadre.

"Waiter could I have the bill please?" Ray asked the thin, short waiter who had been serving them. He served Ray and his wife each time they came to the restaurant.

"Why yes Mr Blue. I hope everything was satisfying for you and your wife?" He asked as he smiled down at them.

"Ronaldo, yes everything was superb. That is why we keep coming here the food is excellent."

"Oh Mr Blue, you are too kind. Thank you and I will be right back with your bill." Ronaldo left the table only to reappear with the bill in hand. Passing it to Ray who dug into his pocket hauling out a small wad of cash making sure not only the bill was paid but a nice twenty dollar tip for Ronaldo.

Leaving the restaurant walking to their car it was now seven-thirty as Ray glanced at his watch. Something off to the left caught his attention. Looking over he saw two bikers sitting on their bikes watching him and his wife. It was the worst feeling as Ray could feel their eyes staring him down as if they were looking right into his soul. If some altercation were to arise from this then the bikers would have them dead cold and before leaving to go to the restaurant, ray had placed his service revolver on his dresser back home.

"Get in the car." He told his wife as he opened the front passenger door for her making sure she was comfortable in the car before he shut the door then walked to the driver side to get in.

"I have this feeling I usually get when I confront someone, not knowing if I am going to make it through." He mentioned to his wife.

"Jesus Ray, you shouldn't talk like that. Its probably just because you're horny." Taking a breath she continued on, " we still have time to kill before we get home to the babysitter, kiddo." She smiled at him hoping Ray would take her up on her proposal. She said it mostly to change the macabre conversation Ray was on. She had been after him for years to leave his work at the office but she knew her husband and he was a cop's cop. By the book she knew he could sense something when it did not appear right. But times were hard all around so who needed the pressure?

"Not tonight. I have some things I have to clear up. I was hoping to work through the night." He told her which really surprised her as this was her first night back and all he had on his mind was work? She needed a good tumble in the hay.

"the hell you say. I want our time to be just that, our time. Christ you give them ten or eleven hours a day, so now you are on my time!" Ray was just not listening. He knew with these urchins in town there was going to be trouble. He had to be prepared when they made their move. This drew back memories for her as she remembered when

Ray was a beat co and how he had flipped out one night because some armed robbery was going down, only thing was the robbers killed the security guard who was Ray's uncle Bert. Needless to say Ray buried the four of them, got all the money back and received a promotion from Corporal to Sargeant. Time has changed since back then. There's so much corruption which goes right up the ladder which is sad in a way because a good cop not only has to worry about the criminals but also their partners.

Ray did not need another argument, not tonight anyways but he knew something was not right, something was wrong and he had to correct it or have it corrected fast or someone else close to him could lose their life.

"You tell me Ray." Claire started.

"Tell you what?"" He asked wondering where this was going.

"You tell me you love me. C'mon say it and don't forget the promises you made with me about your fucking job." Clair said as tears ran down her face. She was a strong backer for her husband but it looked like things were beginning to fall apart between the two of them. Yeah in his own way he loved her but he hadn't had sex with her for nearly a month now because the job kept him away. Now it was their time to be together and was he going to just push it aside again tonight for the job? Claire went on.

"You care more for that fucking job than for me. Here I have tried to support you all these years and now that we have Ray jr am I supposed to be the good wife and take care of him while you go out galavanting around trhying to catch criminals? What about me Ray? What do you think? Just because we had a baby I don't need you anymore? I need you more than ever, especially now. I have plans of growing old with you as we lay together in each other's arms but is that now just a fucking dream?"

Ray pulled over to the side of the road turning off the engine e. he felt like a complete piece of shit, thoughts did go through his mind because yes, he did promise her but he had to clear up this frightening feeling he had deep down.

"listen Clair you know I love you and you are not making the situation any easier. I don't want to do this but I have to because these people in town may be killed because of those fucking bikers. One was killed and for some reason they are holding me responsible. If I don't take the opportunity of clearing this matter up it may cost me my life." He really had to be open with her as she stared back at him in disbelief.

"What are you saying Raay? Is there no one else they can trust to fulfill this problem?" She just wanted to go home but before he started the car again he told her as he stared straight into her eyes.

"No Clair there isn't anyone else out there but me." He drove away from where he had been sitting and as he turned to his street he saw Sherry running down towards him. Getting out of the car he asked,

"What's wrong?" he was feeling uneasy about his son's safety.

"Mr Blue your Captain wants you to call him right away. He has been calling every hour for you." Looking over at his wife Ray told her.

"Claire you go with Sherry in to the house and lock the door. I have to go there and get my gun. Then I have to go." As Clair made her way to her house Sherry spoke up.

"Would you like it if I stayed a little longer Mr Blue?"

"Yes that would be nice if you can. She certainly could use the companionship and please lock the door." A heavy disturbing feeling was in the pit of Ray's gut. Something was out of place and he was the only one who could correct it. Going to the house with the girls Ray ran to his bedroom to gather his gun, vest and plenty of ammunition.

Leaving as fast as he came, Ray jumped in the car heading straight to the station.

Returning to the office was faster than what Ray had expected. It seemed there was no traffic on the streets and good wonder with the bikers in town the townsfolk were smart enough to stay in their homes until this menace breezed away.

Ushering into the Captain's office he became more alarmed with the news the Captain broke to him.

"Ray sit down. You need to hear this information before you run into any of those fucking heathens out there." The Captain said as he leaned into his desk peering at Ray who was listening tentatively.

"Why what's up Captain?" Ray asked wanting to get the information out of the Captain. Ray was about to burst with anticipation waiting for the Captain who was taking his time to explain the situation, with clasped hands the captain went on.

"That fellow who got killed in the shoot out happened to be the Vice President of the UnHoly Ones."

' How the hell would I know that…." Ray tried to explain as the Captain cut him off going on with the explanation.

"it gets better." Taking a deep breath the Captain continued. " These fuckers cut down all the telegraph wires leading out of town so we cannot message for reinforcements and they have blocked the main roads so no one can get in or out until we hand you over to them for Unholy justice."

"Are they fucking insane? How many of these bikers are there?" Ray asked stunned he was being held responsible for the biker's death.

"Well some of the officers have been out and about which is what they need to be doing in a more courageous way, but they told me more bikers poured into the area this evening and there's got to be three or four hundred out there riding around. Rest assured I am not going to just hand you over to these animals but I sent Harrison out to see if he can get to the next county to call in the FBI. I haven't heard from him for a couple of hours and when we call his radio there's no answer."

Ray sat there looking at the floor. What was he going to do now? If he gave himself up then the bikers would kill him for sure but if he stayed put no one knows the damage these bikers would commit in their fun and games. Staying at the station was the most sensible action Ray could concede to as everyone in the station tried to come up with some sort of strategy to defeat these bikers at their own game. The night bled on.

When the sun came up around six in the morning, a bike roared on the desolate streets. It was Teaspoon Jerry sat on his bike outside roaring the engine until he had an audience of cops watching him from their windows. One officer braved the outside to go see what this biker was after. Walking right up to the lone biker the cop asked him.

"What do you want?" he was a little nervous until he second guessed this biker remembering he was a criminal.

"I came to see if you pigs were ready to bargain with the UnHoly Ones."

"Bargain eh? What if we are not ready?"

"Then the UnHoly Ones will do a street by street clean sweep until we find the pig who shot our brother. If we find some young ladies we deem good enough to be with us we will take them along so they can service the boys. If he is here you have ten minutes to send him out." Revving up his bike engine he sat where he was for a moment snickering at the rookie who came out to talk with him. Turning the bike around he was about to leave to return to the Chapter he belonged with when the nervous rookie took out his revolver and shot the biker in the back. Ray could not believe his eyes as why this rookie could have been so stupid to take his gun out in the first place. Now that hje had shot a main biker shit would hit the fan. He looked at the Captain telling him,

"I have to go out there. I have to stop this right now or we all may end up dead." The Captain looked Ray straight in the eyes telling him, " C'mon be reasonable. How far do you think you will go? They will kill you then go on a fucking rampage. Use that small but effective brain of yours. We do not need any martyrs. That stupid fucking rookie sealed it anyways." Getting up from his chair behind his desk he paced the floor a moment then speaking low so only Ray could hear he mentioned.

"They want revenge and they will not stop until they get it but I'll be damned if they think they can come in here and tell us what to do. What they need is a fucking .44 in the head. Each and everyone of them." Sitting back down he started to cool down from his anger. It wasn't his fault the cops were caught off guard with these demands which would never be met but it did fray on everyone's nerves.

Getting up from his seat the Captain opened his office door looking at the officers sitting out before him at their desks, when the Captain saw who he wanted.

"Jocko come in here for a little." James Jocko Jackson was a mean officer who used to be with a gang in Harlem New York. He was a big black man who stood around six six who had enough of the street works when he witnessed plenty of friends die from other gangs. He wanted to use his smarts in bettering the lives of people instead of acting like some punk who thought he was tough. Coming out here he joined the Academy to become an officer which he passed with flying colors. Using his knowledge of the street to help wayward kids lead a more successful life he finally found his niche in life. Coming into the Captain's office he sat at the big mahogany desk beside Ray.

"What's up captain?" Jocko asked as he sat attentive to the Captain's orders.

"Ok the three of us must come up with a solid strategy to damage the strength of these bozos and prover to them they are not as dangerous as they believe they are. We need to get out there in the field to see what we are really up against. Now if you run into any of them don't take any chances get back here pronto because this is our haven. So fix your watches boys and let's set to meet back here at 2:30 am." Jocko spoke up telling Ray something he nor the Captain did not know about him.

"Before I became an officer I had a life which I never really talked about. It was Viet Nam. They want a fight they will get a fucking fight. Some of those bikers fought over there but they have lost their way in life coming back stateside with all the riots to stop the war and never getting congradulations for the tough fight they did to keep America free. These fucker's are gonna wish they were still sucking their mama's hind tits because most of them do not know what war is. Half of them believe there's safety in numbers but when the numbers dwindle their courage goes out the window."

"Did you get anything for being over there?" The Captain asked.

"Yeah I received the Purple Heart which I gave to my mother as a remembrance of me being there. My crew I was with over there were surrounded by a troop of gooks but I helped them get away so they gave me the award. They would have ended up in a Cambodian camp " Jocko was really good when he was over in Nam but tonight he just wasn't good enough.

The Captain looked at his men asking, " are you ready? Ok let's move out." Ray on the otherhand decided after tonight for the sake of his dear wife he would leave being a cop and go into private practice.

CHAPTER IV

"Hey baby, don't be scared. I ain't gonna hurt you, no I wouldn't do that to such a beautiful young lady like you, but then there's my friends." Said Spider. A ferret-faced biker who like his females young as this one was. Not quite fourteen but becoming to be a good looker. Screaming and kicking she couldn't keep them all from her as they ripped her clothes off. Salivating at the fresh, young flesh the bikers got the old ladies to hold her down as each of them had a turn with her.

"That was fine fucking. I really love tight pussy." Spider bragged. Then as the other bikers thanked him for their treats Spider changed the subject looking at the other rooms in the house.

"I wonder who else lives in here." Going up the stairs as quiet as he could Spider peered in to a bedroom staring as he saw the form of a woman lying in bed crying. Going over Spider pulled the blankets off. It was Clair, she was scared shitless and in her crying she had a soft plea.

"Please, please don't hurt me, please I beg you." She uttered out as the tears ran down her face. Spider smiled at her as he told her.

"You don't have to beg pretty mama. I'll give it to you."

"No please my husband is a cop and you'll fry for this." Claire hoped this would scare him off but it only intrigued him.

"A cop you say? What's his name? Maybe he's one of the cops we killed tonight. Spider told her as the fear was plainly seen in her eyes. Slapping her across the face several times Spider grabbed hold of her pajamas top ripping it off then in a hunger he tore at the bottoms not paying attention to her pleas of mercy.

"Tell me pretty lady do you want to meet my friends? I think we should take you and your daughter with us for some fine fucking." Calling his friends they came to his calls looking at the fine piece of ass lying on the bed. One of the Chapter leaders was there among them. His name was Crazy and he didn't get that name for being kind. Looking down at her he told Spider and the rest of the riders, "take them both to the camp for the boys to enjoy."

Clair fought them the best she could then swore at them.

"You fucking animals. What about my baby? Are you just going to leave him here all alone without any care?"

"Baby?" Crazy asked. " Spider you have been wanting a kid for some time now. Take this one and raise him," looking down at Clair he asked, " it's a boy right?" Clair nodded yes then smiling Crazy told Spider.

"Here's your chance to have a son.

"You get your filthy hands away from my son you fucking pigs." Clair raged at them then Crazy did not slap he punched her in the mouth knocking out a couple of teeth.

"Shut your fucking mouth or I'll beat you senseless you stupid bitch." Crazy roared at her as they moved from room to room until they found the baby boy. Picking him up from his crib the girls handed it to Spider who held him in his arms for a few minutes then passed the baby back to one of the girls with them.

"You kow what?" Crazy started as he reached down to pull the blankets off the terrified woman to have a good look as the rest looked on in amusement.

' This bitch will turn a good profit doing movies." Laughing he left the room checking to see if there was anything valuable to get some more cash.

As the bikers grabbed a hold of Clair she fought with them constantly making it hard to take her downstairs out to a waiting van where both her and her babysitter were thrown in. "You bastards will pay dearly for this. My husband will kill every fucking one of you, you fucking cockroachs." She got punched twice in the gut to calm her down a little so they could get her back to the camp and entertain the boys. As Clair started to say something one of the bikers stuck his dirty underwear in her mouth to shut her up. It worked but she gagged at the filth they employed upon her.

"I'm telling you to call your wife Ray. Let her know what the hell is going on but please, be cool about it."

The Captain was on foot patrol back in the seventies. He saw what gangs could do, it wasn't very pretty and if it included family, it could get messy.

"Captain I'm not getting any answer when I call. Something's wrong." Putting his phone back in his pocket he reached out to swing the Captain back so he could talk face to face with him.

"I'm going to take a couple of men with me I have to check out my place because something just isn't right. Claire would answer and besides she has Sherry our babysitter with her." "Okay but be careful." The Captain started as he pointed his finger at Ray right in his face.. I want all of you to wear the vests." Turning to face the small crowd of officers with them the Captain called out in a low voice.

"Donaldson. Kruber you back up Blue. Jackson I want you to ride shotgun. If there is one bit of trouble from those bikers, get your asses bacvk here pronto. Do you hear me?" each officer nodded they heard the Captain.

Arriving at the house no one was around at all. Neighbors might be watching from their windows but no one was coming out. First thing they came up to was the front door was visibly kicked in right off the hinges. The windows were all broken and all the lights were on. Ray ran into the house not caring if some biker were pilfering through his belongings. Crying out Clair's name as he ran upstairs he stopped in his tracks as he saw torn clothes on the floor. Running to the baby's room the baby was gone as well.

"What the fuck?" Ray said out loud. No one was there to greet him or give him warm kisses, no the house was completely empty. Dropping to his knees he began to weep because he knew what those fucking animals would do to his sweet wife or the little virgin Sherry. Rage filled his mind as he took two steps at a time coming down. Jackson tried to stop him from going out and getting killed. They were a team so they had to act like a team if they were going to stop this scourge.

"Let go of me!" Ray screamed at Jackson who held him tighter.

"No man. This is exactly what they want. We will get her back and the kid, but right now we have to work together or they will get away with this killing us in the process." Ray became so distraught he went limp knowing what Jackson said was good advice. Going outside ray roared his pain to the universe. Donaldson and Kruber went canvassing to the neighbors because they may have seen something relevant to what took place. Nobody wanted to get involved as most did not answer their doors.

"You fucking cowards." Ray screamed at the hidden neighbors. One young man came forward to speak about what he saw. His father tried to stop him by hauling him back into the house but the young man broker free running up to the cops.

"Who are you and where do you live?" Kruber asked as he came up to the young man.

"I'm Roger Chandler. I live across the street at 267 Lorna drive, over there." He said pointing to the house across the street but a couple of houses down from being directly across the street.

"It was about an hour ago I tried to phone the Police but the line was dead so I crept up as far as I could taking some pictures and writing down licence numbers. I heard them yelling and hitting the woman who lives here."

"How could you see from over there its rather dark out tonight." Kruber asked.

After I tried to use the phone I grabbed my camera and a pad of paper to w rite down anything the Police could use then when some came out I hid in the bushes over there. Then what looked like one of the biker women came out holding a baby, while three bikers dragged the woman and a younger girl out throwing them into a van.

Donaldson took his time coming over to his partner. He was trying to get some other witnesses to come forward to speak out against the bikers but they were all cowards.

"What have you got here?" Donaldson asked as Kruber faced Roger once more.

"This is Roger Chandler he lives there at 267 Lorna drive. He has come forward with some good evidence against those bikers. Pictures, licence plate numbers and he could be a viable witness ifg this gets to court." Looking at Roger again he told him out flatly.

"You may get a citation for your bravery here. Too bad the rest of the neighborhood would not do the same and follow your lead."

"Yeah they need a good needle of courage shot up their ass." Donaldson added. Roger spoke up which was something the cops did not expect for him to say.

"Hold on. Some of these cowards had their homes broken into and were told if they testified against the bastards who did it would be put away but of course nothing happened to them but probation. Now they live in fear for someone to start some sort of retaliation for the people of this block because they testified. Just goes to show you why they do not want to come forward and have those bikers do the same to them as they did here. Who knows if they get involved you cannot promise they will go to jail like the ones who broke into their homes. They could end up still walking the streets waiting for an opportune time to strike back at the ones who testified against them."

"Then tell me why are you getting involved?" Kruger asked.

"I don't believe what those motherfucker's did tonight should get away with they did tonight. So I came forward to see if you can put an end to these bikers. I have 2 younger sisters I fear for when these bikers ride into town. That is why I am here trying to help." Roger told them as he stood there shaking as the thought of retaliation coming against him was still a possibility.

Jackson and Blue came over to the other officers to see if they had come up with any clues of what took place and if anyone had the balls to step up to the bat to get rid of this vermin in their fair city.. Kruger filled them in on Roger's testimony along with what was written down for licence numbers and of course the camera which would bare the faces of those involved with the terrible event. Blue came over to talk with Roger on a personal basis asking pertinent questions about his wife.

"So you say you saw a lady being taken out of the house? Can you tell me what she looked like and what was she wearing?" Roger recognized Ray knowing he was a cop and probably the husband of that unfortunate woman.

"I saw a dark haired woman who was taken outside and thrown into a white van. She was nude and she started kicking and swinging at them but the bikers beat her until she stopped moving then they brought out a young light haired girl and did the same with her. Then a couple of biker women came out holding a baby by the way they were holding it It must have been a baby. One of the women climbed on a bike starting it while the other one holding the baby climbed on the back and they both disappeared into the night."

It hit Sgt Ray Blue so hard he fell to his knees bawling like a child. After about twenty minutes he stopped crying wiping his eyes from the runaway tears pouring down his face and as Jackson stood beside him helped him back to his feet knowing justice was not an issue here as the cops would pass judgement on all of them. But ray came back to Roger asking a question just to see how far he would go.

"If we get those bastards you saw tonight would you be willing to testify against them?"

"Yeah I will." Roger stated nervously. Then Ray and his partners looked at Roger telling him,

"Thank you for helping us so far. You better go home and lock your doors. We will be in touch later."

Roger turned from them and walked back to his house as the officers watched to make sure he got home safely. Then going back to their car the officers got in and headed back to the station but they did not know the bikers had left someone close by to watch out for witnesses.

As Roger went home the biker followed undetected waiting until the cops got in their car and left. Roger had no idea what was happening but as he locked the door he was in for the night. Roger thought all the bikers had left giving him some leeway to talk with the officers. Sooner was a rather big biker who sat outside Roger's home going through some smaller knives he carried to pick the lock of the front door. Being a pro at breaking into homes it did not take him long to unlock the door. Turning the knob slowly allowed him to open the door without any noise. Walking into the house he saw Roger in the kitchen making a coffee. He was up for the day so the coffee would help him stay awake. Quietly Sooner walked into the house slowly walking up behind Roger without Roger even knowing he was there. With his left hand Sooner grabbed hold of Roger but in his right hand he had his weapon, a steel knife, razor sharp which Sooner ran across Roger's throat. Blood shot out everywhere. Sooner let go of Roger letting him fall to the floor then turning Sooner left the house running across the street where his bike was hidden behind some bushes then climbing on he started his bike revving up the engine allowing the roar of his bike scare people still hidden in their homes, then Sooner made way back to his family of bikers. Back at the station there was a disagreement between the officers on what they should be doing.

"We have to go there and free my wife and my son also the young babysitter who was with my wife when this altercation happened. This is kidnapping and god knows what they have done to them so far. They have to pay for this now. We are just wasting time when we should go free them now!" Ray blared at his fellow officers. He went on. " I want those fuckers to pay and I can't do that sitting around here can I?" Ray paced the floor as he was ready to blow up from the anxiety building up in him. But the other officers were listening to what the Captain had told them. Under no circumstances were they to leave the station until the Captain and the officers with him joined forces. Ray couldn't stop thinking of how his wife wanted him to stay home with her. He did not listen to her figuring he knew what was best. His guilt was making him go crazy with desire to kill every fucking biker he saw. Ray knew the other officers wer3e listening to the Captain and he also knew if they sided with him leaving the station to free Ray's wife they could lose their jobs. He had to wait.

Jocko spoke up to ease the situation with his friend.

"Ray we have to be so very careful with this volatile situation if we want convictions, extra careful is the way we must operate. We have to prove to people that the legal system works not for just a few but for everyone." Legal system eh, Ray snickered then he spoke out.

"I am not going to fuck around here with you, taking my sweet old time. Do you hear me? I want fucking action and I want it now!" at that moment the Captain came up from the basement. It was the place on normal days where the Captain went to have a snooze. He was smiling as he approached his detectives which pushed Ray over the edge.

"I'm glad you find this funny. I quit." Throwing his badge on the desk in front of him he went on,

"I have to go and get her back right now." Captain Lutes had no other choice to make because he could not allow his Sgt to go get himself killed or even worse being captured by the bikers to be tortured.

"I'm placing you under arrest."

Ray told him, " if my wife and child are killed I holding you responsible. You will personally answer for it." The other officers, Donaldson, Kruger and Jackson had no choice to do anything else but take him downstairs in the basement putting him in one of the holding cells. Ray struggled against the grip on him from his fellow officers but it was no use. There were a couple of drunks in cells #2&3 who spoke out when they saw Ray trying to free himself. In cell #4 there was an escapee being held for extradition to Texas where he had escaped from. Placing ray in cell # 6 he certainly wasn't very happy. As he sat on the small bunk he thought of what had transpired, he began hating cops as much as the bikers for the way they were treating him. Ray had to think like the bikers if he were to defeat them at their own Game. He would have to get out of the cell he was in then get his .357 and maybe fake his death to allow him free time to pay back for all the hurt he had to endure.

"Good morning to ya Sarge." Scotty the jailer said. He was an older man who had been the jailer attendant for nearly fifteen years. A stout Irishman who was a no nonsense sort of man who could handle himself quite well as he was once an Irish boxer. His short red hair made him look his age but he was in better shape than some of the constables upstairs in the main room.

"I heard ya had such a fracas last 'een. I sure hope ya wasn't sent here fer too long."

"What time is it Scotty?" Ray asked. " I need to talk to the Captain."

"It'd be 9am sir. The Capin said ya wasn't here long enough if yer were be asking fer him. Said ya have to be settling down abit more. I'm truly sorry Sarge but me got to follow orders."

Ray said nothing more as his anger fuming up in him was becoming more like a passion to harm someone, either the bikers or the ones who called him a fellow officer.

The investigating team were sent by the Captain to talk with Roger about eleven am to get a full written and signed statement from him so they could exercise their right to arrest the ones responsible for the fracass they caused last night. Knocking on the door of Roger's house wasn't bringing any answer and as the door was ajar they decided to enter the premises. As they came in they saw a body lying on the floor in the kitchen. At once Larry Kelsey the head Investigator called out to his companions.

"God dammit we are too late. Call the Forensics here and tell them to bring the meat wagon. Don't touch anything in here until we get the room dusted." Blood was everywhere as the officers stared at the only hope for the bikers to be testified against. When the ambulance finally came. Larry told the driver,

"Take this body to Dr Ryder's office." Dr Ryder had been the towns Pathiologist for over thirty years. Larry also had to call the Captain to let him know the sad news.

"Captain this is Larry Kelsey. We arrived at the house around eleven and knocked but there was no answer. With the door partly open we entered the home to find that your witness was killed in the kitchen sometime last night. He had his throat slit. Blood is covering the walls and floor. I ordered the officers not to touch anything until forensics has a chance to check everything out and I called an ambulance to have the body sent over to Dr Ryder's office." The Captain said nothing so Larry continued,

"it now looks like it is going to be nearly impossible to prove the bikers had a hand in what occurred. We have lost the only true witness we had. I know you locked Sargeant Blue up last night but I believe you should release him because now you are going to need his anger to get these damn animals from walking away from all of this."

"Yes you have a point Larry. I have to go down and talk with him." With that the Captain hung up then looking at his closed door from behind the desk he was sitting at, he stood up coming around the desk he reached for the door to open it. When it was open he looked at the mess of officers milking about the room so he snapped at them.

"What do you think this is a social club? Get the fuck to work!" Captain Lutes headed for the stairs leading to the holding cells in the basement. He had no other choice than to talk with Sgt Blue hoping he had settled down a little so he could release him.

"Good Morning Ray." The Captain said as he watched Ray look up at him with a cynical look on his face, Ray said nothing.

"I'm letting the FBI get the job done. I should have gotten in contact with them last night maybe that kid that came forward would still be alive..." Ray cut him off.

"What do you mean still alive? He's our only material witness."

"Yes, yes, I know. That is why the Federal boys have to take care of this. If I let you out you have to promise to let them do their job and not to interfere with their investigation, what do you say?"

Ray answered positively just to get out of the cell because in his bones he really wanted to go and kill as many bikers as he could.

"Okay. I know they will be thorough. Why the FBI and not the State Troopers?"

"Because they found officer Jackson last night. He was tortured then shot repeatedly. I was forced to call in the FBI as now it's a federal issue."

"Fuck!" Ray blurted then again he stated, " Fuck! Did they find my wife and child yet?" Captain lutes did not answer Ray but turned to face Scotty telling him,

"Scotty open the cell and let Sgt blue out."

"I know what you are feeling like" Captain lutes mentioned but Ray set him straight.

"What the fuck do you know? You know sweet fuck all about the way I am feeling and you'll never know how I am feeling." They left the holding cell area going back upstairs to the Captain's office. Once inside the office the Captain reached into his desk drawer hauling out Ray's badge and placing it before him on the desk.

"What do I want that for?" Ray started. " You can keep it for some sort of reminder of how I was treated."

"No you better take it. Take a couple of weeks off and think this through. You're putting everything you worked so damn hard for on the line here just follow my advice and leave it alone. The federal boys will make sure this is done properly. Go home and I will call you when any news comes in." Ray turned and left his office, when he came upon his own desk he opened the top left drawer where he kept a spare .38 taking it he shoved it in his jacket pocket along with a small case of cartridriges. Ray did not need the federal boys. He decided to do this on his own and rid the world of the unholy ones.

CHAPTER V

Ray did not say another word to anyone even if someone said anything to him because they no longer existed with his train of thoughts. Gathering up all his belongings he had at the station Ray realized he would never be coming back. His days of being a cop were about to end so he had to go home to what was left for him to endure with and figure out a plot, carry it out and never return. Picking up his monitor for the computer he looked at it seeing the glass was cracked then looking down as something caught his eye, it was the wedding picture of him and Clair. Tears ran down his face as he thought of what those bikers were doing to her. Man they would pay for messing up his life. Turning on the computer ray then plugged in the monitor hoping it would work. It did but the images displayed were a little fuzzy so taking a few moments he thought of what he wanted to look up. After fiddling with it for ten minutes he finally reached what he wanted. The airport had destination and arrival times so booking a flight to Hawaii for in the morning, he got his confirmation saved it to his computer then turned the computer off. Heading into the kitchen Ray reached under the cupboard hauling out a half full bottle of Jack Daniels. Taking a long drink from the bottle he realized he needed that. Looking around he saw the bikers had tried to damage everything like the stove, the refrigerator and even his television in the den. Smiling Ray knew he would damage them Going into .the bedroom where he had found Clair's torn clothes he went to the closet hauling out a small duffle bag then, going to his dresser he threw in some underwear, socks, light shirts and an extra pair of jeans. He had everything down to a tee as to what he had to do. The other officers had heard Ray talk about his war buddy but never met him and that was okay with his buddy who wanted to stay secluded. His name was Mike Janid and he was an explosive expert. So he had to go see him about getting some support for the meeting with the bikers. Leaving his home he went to his car throwing his duffle bag on the back seat then closing the back door Ray opened the driver's side and got in. He sat there for a moment to regain his thoughts then started the car. Putting the car in reverse he slowly backed out of his driveway. Heading over to Mike's place he took his time even driving past his house then walking back to not draw any attention he was visiting Mike. Ringing the doorbell it took a few minutes before a short stocky individual answered.

"Hello Ray. How are you doing? C'mon in." Mike exclaimed as he held the door open for his friend. Ray walked straight in.

"I heard about your family man. If there's anything you need at all I got your back."

"Thanks Mike. How did you find out what took place?"

"Aw shit man its all over the news. Terrible thing to take place but here in this shithole of a town. Are they going after those fucking creeps?"

"That's just it Mike. They sit on their asses at the station like nothing happened and tell me to take a couple of weeks off. Can you imagine."

"Holy shit I can't believe they aren't going after them. What the fuck?"

"Exactly. Well I'm not letting them get away with this. That's why I came to see you. I need some power to take them on."

"Whatever you need man."

"I'm going to need some C-4 about a pound."

"Shit man what are you going to do blow up the whole fuclking town?"

"If that's what it takes." Ray browsed around the house but was taken downstairs where the hardware was.

"Okay I can supply the C-4 but it's fucking expensive. I will cut uyou a good deal if you help me get off those drug charges, you know, talk to Jocko, what do you say?"

"Yeah I can squash them. But I'm going to need a good automatic rifle that doesn't jam and five clips of armor piecers."

"the best machine gun ever made is the AK47. Its Russian and I only have six clips left. You may as well take them all. That last clip might come in handy when five may n ot be enough."

"Okay I will take them. How much is all this going to cost? And you better give me a few grenades. Do you still have those Glocks?"

"Yes." Mike answered looking at his friend then asked him, " are you planning to start a war?"

"No. Finish one."

"Well let me figure out how much this is with the discount. I'll be right back. Ray watched him leave the room then called out to him.

"Hey Mike?" Mike came back into the room to see what Ray wanted and wished he hadn't because the air was so cold and stiff enough to cut it with a knife.

"You call me?"

"We have a deal here but don't fuck me around or let anyone know what I plan on doing or you will never be found."

"Shit man what do you take me for? I'll be right back." Leaving the room once again he went to another room upstairs. Ray got a weird feeling so going upstairs he saw his friend talking on the phone. Ray could not believe this guy. Listening in he heard him talking with the Police. He waited for Mike back downstairs ot letting on he heard enough to kill this guy.

"Okay gather up all that I asked for and I will pay you more than thsat." Mike scurried around gathering what him and Ray had agreed on then placing it all on the table in the center of the basement. Ray made on he was going for his wallet but pulled out his .357 magnum.

"What the hell is this?" Mike asked as his voice was warbly. His fear was no hidden secret.

"I was upstairs listening you talk to the cops, you fucking rat. Here I was trusting you with my life and you cut my throat." Ray pulled back the hammer. Mike was shaking but tried to explain his course.

"Ray you can't go after those guys half-cocked. I don't want you getting hurt that's why I made the phone call."

"Getting hurt? You're the fucker who's gonna get hurt." Ray said as he fired a round into mike's chest. Walking over to him he aimed the gun at the already dead corpse in front of him firing another round into his head for safety sake. Gathering up his arms and ammo Ray went back upstairs to the kitchen area with an arm full of weapons and asmmo. Setting everything down on the kitchen table he looked around and found what he needed in the hall closet, an army duffle bag which was much bigger than anything they sold at the stores. Filling it up Ray was about to leave but thought once more in the basement might prove healthy for him. He was right. Off to the left was another small room with an opened safe in it. Ray bent down to take a look at the contents, there sitting in plain view were two stacks of hundred dollar bills. Scooping them up he shoved them into his pockets. This might come in handy being on the street which meant what he had planned with the explosive would make it so easy to disappear because if he used his bank card for anything the cops could put a trace on him. Going back to the kitchen ray grabbed the large duffle bag slinging it over his shoulder then he left Mike's place. It was good he drove and parked further down the street because as he was reaching his car, flashing lights of two cop cars pulled up in front of Mike's home. Smiling Ray started up his car and drove away.

As Ray drove for a few minutes out of the area, he pulled over to a parking spot beside the curb then took the money out of his pockets and began counting it. He had made a good choice of taking what was in the safe, $5000.00 sat there beside him. He knew he had to kill the trail behind him this was another reason why Mike had to die. Leaving the money on the seat beside him he moved out of his parking spot heading straight for the airport. He had a plan in progress which would give him clearance to do what he had to do to make this all come true from a bad dream to vengeance on the bikers and a cleansing of the animals who made his life a sheer spot of thin ice. There were times ray thought about killing himself but what good would that do? No, these bikers had to pay for the crimes and agony they caused normal people who were really law abiding citizens. Pulling up to the parking area at the airport, Ray parked far in the back so he would not be detected on what he was planning. Getting out of the car he took the bag containing the ammo, then reaching in to it he pulled out the C-4 with detonators. He learned when he was in the war to make bombs. It was a trait he never forgot as he remembered the disfigured people he used them on. Many died but those who were unfortunate to live became disfigured for life. They could not afford to have themselves repaired so had to keep on living with not only pain from the burns but the pain that looked hideous for the rest of their lives. He really thought of blowing those fucking bikers from here to kingdom come. First things first. He called the Captain letting him know he had booked a flight to Hawaii and asked to see him before the plane left. When the Captain did meet up with Ray they went out for a few beers because in his heart, Ray knew he would never see the Captain again. As he waited for the Captain, Ray put his duffle bag through the checkpoint so it would be taken on the plane. One less headache to worry about. It also gave Ray a free hand to get done what needed to be worked on. The reason he also wanted the Captain to have a few drinks with him was he knew the Captain got tipsy after three beers.

"I know we had our disagreements." Ray began, " but I also know you saw the future of me getting into trouble and I want to thank you for looking out for me even though at the time I was in a bad way. This trip will do me a world of good to get the pain out so I can live my life with the one I love no matter what took place with what she had to endure."

"now that's the spirit." The Captain replied. " You see I look after all my men and let them see the harm it can cause if they do not do as I suggest." Ray gave a phony smile as he raised his glass to his Captain clinking them together. Standing Ray told him, " I have to use the washroom. I will be right back.," But Ray did not come back leaving the bill with the Captain to deal with. Leaving the airport he made his way back to his car then got in. He just sat there looking at his watch to see when the plane was ready to take off. Then starting the car up he drove like a mad man down a dirt road which would leave him at the end of the runway. Parking his car he waited until the roar of the jet passed over head before getting out of the car then taking the little switch out of his pocket he aimed it at the plane as it started to reach the clouds. Pressing the switch was the avenue of starting the countdown for the bomb to detonate. The plane would be over the Pacific ocean when it happened so all trace of him being on the plane was circumstantial from a drunk Captain who was with him the final moments before getting on the plane and of course the airline itself would have record he had bought a ticket. The bomb was due to go off in just over an hour giving Ray plenty of time to get concentrated here on the ground. There was no turning back now that the die had been set. Looking at his watch it was a quarter to three. He needed some sleep so finding a secluded area hidden by plenty of trees and bushes he parked the car then letting the seat fall down backwards as far as it could go, Ray got comfortable then closed his eyes. The silence allowed him to fall asleep straight away. Waking suddenly, Ray had to get his thoughts together as to why he was in a car in the woods. It all came back to him but the super snooze he had helped him quite abit. Turning the car on he also pulled his seat back into its proper position Ray left the area. As a precaution he turned on his radio to see if there were any news reports about the plane going down. Fiddling with the radio he tried to get into the FBI"s airways to see if they had any report of the plane.

"Have a thought for Lt Staver. Please advise him of this information pronto. I will be at the Black Diamond club this evening around eight. Tell him to meet me there to go over the information, do you copy?"

"Ten-four copy. Base out."

Ray shook his head. " Lt Staver." Ray kept repeating to himself because that name hit a spot with him because he knew that name. then it came to him.

Ray had the right airport and he knew that fuck-faced Staver was in charge of the investigation. Ray would go to the club himself to see what he could find out. Before going he had to prepare himself not to be recognized so his long hair had to go. Ray decided to shave his head and take his moustache off so he would not be easily recognized. If need be later on he could grow them again. Of all the dirty shitfaced fuckers, why him. Ray kept questioning himself. Suddenly it came across what he was hoping for.

"There was a large explosion over Crawlfish Station. I need everyone to put their ears on." This was a small place just on the way of leaving the mainland heading out over the Pacific Ocean,

"All those listening to this distress please copy." The radio shared over a hundred officers coming to "copy" their intentions of helping out. It had worked as Ray carefully drove down the highway getting out of town heading to where the bikers were last seen until on the radio a report came in.

"car Fiver do you copy? Car Fiver please come in."

"Sorry about that just getting a coffee. What's up?"

"There are reports in your vicinity of a group of Unholy Ones partying it up at Willow Creek. I want you to go investigate but do not approach. Wait for back-up."

Ray started over there on his own when a car passed him probably doing eighty. Ray saw a biker in the loaded car so he began to follow which was rather simple Along the way the road had bushes on either side making the road more like a small lane. This was a good strike of luck for Ray as he had no clue where to start his search. The hell with Staver and his information. Here Ray had the opportunity to off some of these bastards before cops came to investigate. Parking the car off the laneway ray had an AK-47 with him and a couple of clips . Cutting through the trees of the winding lane Ray saw some bikers sneak up on a car where a guy and girl were trying to make out. Opening the door of the car Ray saw the bikers pull the guy out of the car beating him while others helped themselves to the girl. Her screams only made the situation worse as the bikers enjoyed inflicting terror on the young woman before they were finished. Ray lifted his gun ready to fire whenever he needed with the bikers preoccupied with the game they were playing now so he moved in for the kill.

"hey Rook. Toss me over a couple of beers. " Came a voice from beside the car.

"Come get it yourself. Who was your nigger last year." Was the answer which brought reprecussions as a fight broke out between the two. Ray took advantage of this, as all the bikers were watching the fight, no one was watching the road.

"hi fellas? How ya doing?" Ray asked as he leveled the gun on them and opened fire. He killed the ones he thought to be the most dangerous first blowing the kneecaps off the ones he wanted to question.

"What do you want man?" I didn't do anything to you. My god look at the blood. Rook answer me, for fucksakes you killed Rook. You better kill me or so help me if I get the chance I'll make you bleed."

"that sounds like a really wise decision." Ray said as he lowered the gun on the unwary biker.

"Hey man I was just joking around, you can take a joke can't you?"

"Sure I can but not today." Ray said as he fired the gun killing the crippled biker. Ray looked over to his right seeing four young girls who looked like they were no older than thirteen at the very most their faces were loaded down with make-up so they could be used for sex with other men also being whores for the bikers themselves.

"Tell me girls, you like what you see?" Ray began. One of the girls piped up in defense of the bikers.

"Yeah well, when Crazy gets a hold of you, we'll tell him everything you did to us and our men."

"You call this shit men?" Ray asked as he pointed to the dead bikers strewn across the lot. " I want you two over by the tree and you two up here by me to take this rawhide and tie your friends face first to this tree up here beside me." No one moved. Then Ray yelled at them.

"Get your fucking asses moving now. Pronto or I'll cut your fucking heads off!" They picked up the pace moving as fast as they could as they saw Ray was not afraid to kill. So obeying him they tied the two remaining bikers face first to the tree. It was a giant spruce tree with gum running down the side. Taking a canteen Ray poured water on the wrists of the bikers with hopes the sun would shrink the leather making it tighter for the bikers. Looking at the girls the one who had defended the bikers was standing close to Ray so he grabbed her tearing her jeans off throwing her to the ground as she fought him putting up a good battle but Ray overcame her kicks and scratches getting the better of her then toying with her a little he raped her. As she lay on the ground siveling he watched the horror of the other young girls as he picked up his gun, leveled it at the girl's head and squeezing off a shot. Turning to the other girls he walked over to them letting them know what was waiting for each of them.

"This is what is going to happen to each of you if you don't tell me what I want to know." Looking at what seemed to be the youngest, Ray looked at her asking with his eyes but it did not go the way he wanted. They would suffice taking care of her better than anything he could come up with. Making a small incision on her left arm the blood dripped on the ant hill. The ants began to scurry around trying to find where this commodity was coming from. Investigating they began to crawl all over her biting her leaving little marks on her. She woke in pain crying out to Ray.

"Oh god. please, please kill me. I can't stand this terrible feeling of having bugs all over me biting me." It too about ten minutes before she passed out again. Ray smiled as he looked over at the last two.

"I have something nice planned for you two. If you are not into pain then I suggest you better do some talking."

"I know who you are," volunteered Therese. She was a cute redhead. " You're that fucking cop who killed my boyfriend Ricardo. You can go fuck yourself." Ray turned to the other girl hoping she had a lick of sense to see he wasn't fucking around. Walking over to the mouthy one Ray punched her in the head three or four times. Looking at the last one she was crying as she blurted out, " I was kidnapped by these animals. All I want is to go home to my family." The one who got punched looked at her telling her,

"Don't tell him he lit the pile. She felt a warm sensation at first but the pain of her feet being cooked she screamed at the unbearable pain. The pain made her go off the deep end but this was the kind of torture this anything. He can't be told where the rest are. He just can't be told. We will win if we stick together. Don't be like him a fucking rat." Ray walked over to her with his knife in his hand he bent down lunging at her with the knife, stabbing her three, four times as the last breath left her body. Turning back to the one who was crying he waited for a moment before untying her. She rubbed her wrists trying to get circulation back in them then as she got to her feet dshe lunged at Ray trying to get his gun. Ray grabbed her before she could reach it. Taking her by the hair he beat her until she passed out unconscious. Ray was really mad now, Grabbing her so when she came to the world of the living he looked at her with a strange look in his eyes. She knew at that moment she was going to die. Ray gathered some branches and small twigs Ray dragged her to a tree picking her up he tied her to the tree a couple of feet off the ground. Placing the branches and twigs under her feet was made for. Ray did this to his prisoners in the war, it was effective, doing the job completely. Watching her writhe around in pain Ray told her, " I need to know where the rest are holed up. If you don't tell me I will continue to torture you." This was not working the way Ray hoped it would. Here four girls and six bikers were dead and now he had to let this one die as well. As he turned away from her he caught some movement in the bushes. Going to pick up his rifle then making his way over to the bushes Ray was totally surpised to see a biker taking a shit.

"Looking for the ass wipe buddy?" Being taken off-guard like this Romero tried to run away with his pants down around his ankles. It did not help much but this allowed Ray to have another hostage for questioning.

Bringing him to the place where he had started the fire under the young girl. He caught her trying to put the fire out because the rope he tied her feet with burned away. Stomping the fire with her already burnt feet must have really hurt but it was better than losing her life. Ray watched her for a moment with the biker he captured. She looked over seeing Romero sitting on the ground with Ray's automatic rifle resting against his head. .Looking down at the biker he told the young girl.

"Nice guy you befriended here. He sat in the bushes watching you girls die. Now that's what I call a friend you're willing to die to protect."

She could not believe what she just heard. Getting herself down from the tree she had to get on her hands and knees to move around slowly. She started crawling over to the biker who looked like hell as he saw all the dead bodies around the camp knowing his life was not worth anything to this cop.

"So you were hiding in the bushes while this fucker was killing us? What kind of a shithead are you anyways? If we get out of this I'm telling Crazy everything. I want to be able to watch you get beaten to death, yeah, that's what I want." The biker turned to her to tell her the truth.

"who the hell do you think you are? You are nothing but a tramp to keep our beds warm and make us money. Go tell Crazy, all he will do is laugh in your face. We can get whores when we need them so big deal those other whores died. You are just an expendable tramp.' Coming up close to him she slapped him even biting him as the biker tried to stop her blows. The turning to face the girl again Ray asked..

"Tell me where the other bikers are." She looked Ray up and down then told him ."Go fuck your mother." Ray was amazed by her courage but there was a price to pay for her courage. Picking up a smoldering stick from the fire Ray stuck it in her eyes blinding her. Then he left her where she was. Turning to the biker he started with him.

"Romero is it? I want some answers pal and I want them now or you will forfeit your life as well.

"You know yourself eventually I will find the camp. So why tolerate the pain I will inflict to save your buddies? Comprenda senor. Tell me what happened to Officer Jackson, how did he die?"

"I do not understand what you mean or who this Officer Jackson is." Romero answered mockingly.

Ray was going to just sit back and enjoy this fellow dying. Ray did not want to kill the young girls but he had no choice. Again he questioned Romero.

"Tell me Romero who killed Officer Jackson?"

"I do not know senor. I did not meet the man you are talking about."

"Never met the man eh? Then tell me Romero, how is it you got the very boots on thsat belonged to Officer Jackson? If you never met him who gave them to you?"

"Ok I got them from my old lady you seemed to have killed so I guess she died with the answer." He told Ray laughing.."

"Well yes I killed everyone here so that is the same that is going to happen to you if you don't start talking."

"I don't believe you will kill me senor. You are a cop and you can't lkill."

"Oh is that so? Well I suggest you talk to those dead ones over there because you are about to join their numbers.

"Hey man maybe you need a vacation. Your job must be really stressing you out." Ray had enough of the bullshit so reaching under the chair he had made out of a couple of the bodies he hauled out the head of Cindy, who happened to be a favorite of Crazy. Tossing it over to Romero, it landed in his lap. . Romero cried out in fear knowing this cop was going to kill him if he talked or if he didn't. So to make matters harder for the cop he was not going to talk and rat out on his friends. Standing Ray dragged the cuffed biker who had his hands cuffed behind his back to he spot where the car was. It was a bit of a struggle because they had to go through some rough underbrush to reach the car. Ray opened the trunk then picked up the biker and threw him in. Getting into the car himself Ray checked the clip in the AK-47 to see if he needed a new clip. It was alright then taking out his .357 Magnum he set it on the seat beside him incase he needed fire power right away. Once out of the area of the forest he drove just inside the city limits to a garage . So as he pulled into the driveway he knew had a steel fence in behind, parking beside it Ray cared little about the biker in the trunk, so laying down like he had done before by putting the seat backwards, he closed his eyes for some shuteye. A rap on his window woke him up, as he sat there yawning, he looked out the window. Reaching for his gun, it wasn't there. He saw where it was.

"Okay cop get out of the car now." Coaster commanded Ray to get out as Ray tried in vain to get his thoughts together. Looking at the Biker as he opened the door to get out. " Fuck off." This did not help his situation in the least.

"I have been hearing you want a conference with me pig. What do you want to talk to me about? Sports, the weather, maybe you want to tell me what you did to Cindy." Laughed the strong stenched biker who really needed a good cleaning shower. Ray did not back down from any of them as he blurted out.

"I just want to know where that goon called Crazy has been hiding. What's wrong with him? He has to hide behind you guys showing he's nothing but a coward. Each time I get close to him he goes into hiding." The bikers looked at Ray then approached him with kicks and punches. Ray swung back but there were too many of them to contend with. When he got out of the car he tried to hit one on them with the car door but they had wrestled him to the ground. Finally from the beating he received he passed out. Yes he was out cold in his enemy's hands.

As Ray began to wake up he was in unfamiliar territory. Then he realized he himself was now a prisoner in a very small room for him. There was hardly enough room to get up from the cot he was lying on. Ray tried to get up but couldn't. He was tied to the cot so tight he could only move his head. When the

"Well it's about time you came back to earth. I have places to go so you wanted to talk with me. My name is Crazy do you happen to know why they call me Crazy? It's because I do not take shit from anyone, I earned my respect with this group and I understand you want to change that, well, you have to take a number but the last guy did not fare too well". The dirty biker laughed at his own words.

Ray was taken off guard but he let him know why he was after the son of a bitch.

"You're the mother fucker who killed my wife and stole my son.."

"So what i.f I did, what are you going to do about it?" snickered the biker. Turning around he told two other bikers, " Untie him and take him to the field of honor, we will see if this cop is really tough enough to withstsand what we have planned for him

The Field of Honor was a pit twenty feet feet wide and the same in length. It ran to ten feet deep which looked ominous at first which got Ray a little scared as to what was going to happen to him so he asked.

"What happens here?"

"You'll find out." One of the whores answered as all the bikers and whores standing around the pit were laughing and carrying on while they smoked pot and drank booze. Crazy stood up cowering over Ray as he told him.

"Okay cop. Here is where you can prove your law is better than biker law. If you win you can walk out with this little bitch right here. You know her as your babysitter. We took her to give her more worth and man she has a tight little body the boys really enjoyed. Now if you win you can leave here with this little honey and in the future if you still think its worthwhile to come after me, well by all means come after me. But as you can see by your capture, I am not one to trifle with." As the bikers grabbed hold of Ray on each side of him they threw him in the pit. Looking at his babysitter the bikers snickered and laughed amongst themselves as they found enjoyment in the fear she was in.

Ray stood in the pit trying to prepare himself for the game the bikers were playing. Then Crazy spoke once more.

"I have to say goodbye for now but if you need a reference for later in life maybe as a stripper, I do have the right connections and I could give her a good recommendation." Again everyone laughed some even whistled as ray stood there wishing he had been more careful while he was in the car.

"Oh one other thing. If you lose you die. Here meet your opponent, his name is Fixer and you'll find out why he is called that." Ray thought if he could get his hands on this Crazy he would tear him apart but right now he had his plate full when his opponent came into the pit. He was a giant of a man, he stood six-eight and looked like he weighed three hundred pounds. As soon as the Fixer made a play to grab hold of Ray, Ray kicked him hard in the groin. Fixer stood there as if nothing happened. Then Ray gave him a haymaker which would have knocked anyone else into the promised land but it did nothing to Fixer who did not even flinch. Ray knew he was in trouble and had to think of something to bring this giant down. Fixer was black and Ray knew blacks had weak shins so maybe this was his call to glory as Ray put all his power he had left into his right foot standing on his left and kicked Fixer in the shin just below the knee. Fixer dropped to his knees trying to protect his face from the kicks Ray was sending him.

Sgt Ray Blue was getting good at landing blows with his feet. Ray surmised even if he lost this nigger was getting something he would remember from this day. Seeing his enforcer was in deep trouble, Crazy jumped into the pit to help his comrade. Ray noticed this so he pushed Fixer on his back making sure he could connect with Crazy with a kick to the nuts. It landed squarely making Crazy think he was getting spayed. Calling out to his mates some jumped into the pit to help out because this was going sour with Fixer and Crazy being down for the count.

"You're a stupid fucker, cop, if only you let him take you down, it would have been fast and painless. But no, you had to prove yourself that you're such a tough son of a bitch. Well now you lose by breaking the rules."

"What fucking rules?" Ray roared at him, " There are no fucking rules." Seeing there was no chance for him while in the pit, Ray tried to climb out but was hauled back in.

"Where do you think you're going?" Fixer asked Back in the pit laying on his back, Ray was being kicked so much it gave his body a different sensation. He felt really different, light as if he died. This is what the bikers thought. Too bad they did not take better recognition leaving him for being dead. Ray felt like he was floating on the air.

CHAPTER VI

Waking up slowly Ray thought he would never experience such a beating again. He really thought he was a goner but trying to remember what he had gone through it kept filling his mind of him falling down slowly then as if some invisible being was carrying him off, floating on the air.

The sun was at high noon. The light was blinding him as he tried to open his eyes and get a bearing of where he was. Remembering the pit he was in he rolled over on his stomach to try to push himself to his knees then eventually to his feet. He passed out again. When he awoke again it was evening. The cool air felt better than having the sun beat down on him. His head was thumping which made it hard for him to open his eyes. But once again he was on his knees trying to push himself into a standing position which he did but lost his balance so he reached out to the side of the pit to hold him up. How would he get out of here? Looking around the whole pit he realized it was not so deep at the other end, about six feet which if he could manage he would pull himself out. It took almost all his strength to grab hold of whatever he could pulling himself free from this pit. Once out he lay where he was for a few minutes then making sure he was clear of the pit so he would not fall back in, he dragged himself away. Again he got up this time though he knew he needed some sort of sustenance as his stomach growled for food. Leaving the area. Ray remembered where the car was parked. It was quite a little hike but he had to get back to it because if it were still there he had some peanuts, chips and a couple of cokes stashed in the trunk for emergencies. This was an emergency. It took him about two hours of moving through the forest towards the car which under better circumstances would have taken fifteen minutes but he had to stop every little while to catch his breath by leaning against a tree. Finally spotting the car there seemed to have someone sitting in the front passenger seat so he was wary when approaching the car. Ray did not give a fuck as to the time he was on borrowed time from what had happened to him and as he came up close to the car he peered in through the passenger window to see something most disgusting. There on the front seat was Sherry his babysitter. He grimaced as what those fucking animals had done to her. Yes she was dead. Sherry was a beautiful girl full of life who had said on numerous occasions she wanted to be a model. Here she sat naked and humiliated. Ray thought of her working each day after school as a waitress to help her mom pay the over loading bills that her father had left when he ran out on the family leaving them to fend for themselves. The bikers had cut off her tits, cut her tongue out and shoved a two by two up her pussy. She looked like she had been dead for four days. Sitting beside her for the night. He had adjusted the seat so he could lay down and fall asleep, he couldn't do it until he put something in his belly so getting out was a chore but he did. The bikers had left the keys in the ignition and before getting out he tried to start the car but it would not turn over so he used the keys to open the trunk. In there he found a small bag of nuts, a mars bar, a bag of stale chips and two bottles of warm coke. Ray had a hard time chewing but he had to endure the pain to get something in his belly. Each time he swallowed he vomited. It helped drinking the warm coke but the sweetness was disturbing to his gut. It was enough. The food he tried but kept him getting sick enough to vomit so he decided to go back and lay don in the car. Trying to get the car door open it took him longer as his swollen hands hurt as he had to push in the button to get inside. Once opened Ray looked at Sherry thinking about how bubbly she was to him and his wife. She was the one who really looked after his son, his son, where could he possibly be? Sliding into the seat. Ray half-turned in his seat to pull the blanket from the back seat to cover himself up. He was shaking from chills and wanted to make sure he would feel better in the morning. Sticking the keys into the ignition once again he tried to turn the engine over but it failed like before. Turning it back he closed his eyes as he lay there and passed out. Morning came with the sun high in the sky telling Ray it maybe close to ten am. Getting out of the car he heard something he did not notice before. There was a silence in the air except for a faint noise off to his left. Going towards the sound it was a babbling brook so going to it he dropped to his knees at what seemed like a deep part of the brokk falling face first into the cold water. The magic of the cold water woke him up more than what he was. Pushing himself up letting the cold water run over his swollen hands felt good. Now he was more intuned to do what needed to be done. Going back to the car Ray opened the hood of the car to take a look at the engine noticing the distributor cap was missing. Searching around the car he could not find it. So going over to the passenger side of the car he opened the door getting g a good hold of Sherry he tried to lift her up but found every time he touched her skin she stuck to him meaning regimortise had set in. Taking off his shirt he ripped it in two wrapping each piece around his hands then grabbing hold of her, he carried her to the pit letting her drop into it. Going back to the car he felt something like a lump sticking in his back so reaching under the seat he hauled out the head of Cindy. Those fucking beasts had beheaded the dead girl leaving her head with him as a fond remembrance of her. Tossing her head into the bushes towards the pit. Ray fell down beside the car noticing something just under the car, it was the distributor cap. Pulling it out from under the car he used the car to regain his composture then taking the cp to the engine he fitted it back on hopin g the car would finally start. Before getting back into the car, Ray's gut was rumbling. He needed a good crap so right where he stood he dropped his pants and let nature take it's course. It hurt at first but he felt a little better when it was finally finished. Now he got into the car, he had to open all the windows because the smell of death was now in the car. The seats carried the scent of death which was really overwhelming. He wondered how doctors who had to perform autopsies could handle this smell. With the car running properly Ray started down the lane knowing where he had to go to reach a pharmacy. Remembering in the lining of the seat he was on he pulled the car over ripping open the seat showing something that brought a smile to his face. There before him was a small cylindrical tube. It contained one thousand dollars for an emergency. Ray now knew he was going to kill everyone who was on the side of the Unholy Ones. For all they did in killing his family, his friends, fellow officers these dirty fuckers had to be repaid. They only caused grief and death in anything someone cherished in every path they took thinking they were not accountable for their actions because unbeknownst to the general public they were above the law, having a law for themselves which boiled down to the good of the bike group and the hell with everything else. Ray was getting closer to his destination, the pharmacy. It was going to be a tricky situation as the pharmacy was right next door to Pete's restaurant as both were in the same building. Pete's was a regular watering hole for most of the officers on the force so he had to be extra careful going in getting what he wanted then get out without being recognized. As Ray parked the car he took a deep breath knowing this had to be done. His side ached, his hands were cramping up so to make sure he had medical attention he had to get some necessities to help him deal with his pain. Going inside he was fortunate because he was the only one there besides a young boy at the cash register. Going straight to the aisle carrying antiseptics, Ray decided to grab a couple bottles of pain killers to help him subside the pain. Paying for them he turned and let the pharmacy without a hitch. He did not want to take a pain killer on an empty stomach so he went to a drive thru fast food shop and ordered a couple of hamburgers with fries and an iced tea. He needed the nourishment in his belly to stop it from growling then when he finished that chore Ray headed back to the forest he woke up from this morning. No one would be looking for him there nor the bikers. Yet with all the trouble they were causing Ray could not believe these cops were doing nothing about it. They were in for a rude awakening he thought to himself when they would find bikers and those on the side of the bikers dead. Now what he needed was to sit quietly for another day to think things out. It was not going to hurt his plans but the needed rest would do wonders for him. One thing he needed was a gun and ammo since the bikers stripped the car down for any weapon they found which meant they had his C-4, the detonators, his AK-47 and the clips. They wanted a war, they were about to get one.

While at the place where the bikers left him for dead, Ray scoured the area looking for some semblance of a weapon. There was none. He remembered Charlie's bait shop in the next county. Charlie was an old war vet, much older than Ray, but he had a stash of relics from the war and also some new weapons which could prove quite successful if he had them. Squatting above the pit where he had placed Sherry, Ray said a little prayer for her promising to repay these terrible people for what they did. People? They weren't people, no they were animals who cared little for human life. Tears flowed down his cheeks as he thought of his wife and the terrible shit she had to endure with these bastards. Then his son, where the hell could he be? Did they sell him to somebody who couldn't have kids or would they keep him teaching him all their mindless, dirty traits? Wiping his eyes with the back of his hand Ray stood up then in an instance facing the skies let out a roar of pain which seemed to empty all the hurt out of his soul, letting him come to the understanding if a cop crossed his path to try to stop him then the cop would have to die. Nothing would deter Ray from accomplishing his main purpose in life, get rid of the Unholy Ones and the women who seemed to be as depraved as they were.

Going back to the car Ray checked his gas gauge. He had a quarter tank so getting gas was a priority but as he sat in the car it came to his realization that the smell of death was a strong odor which was not good for him. He had to change cars. He loved the innocence of Sherry but the stench of death was all around him. It took his thoughts to a different plane not being to really think of a plot to enact but made his thoughts dwell on the shit the bikers had caused. Backing up he drove down the lane trying to think of a place to get rid of this car and taking one. A thought came to him. The Police station. Each car there either a cop car or civilian had a two-way radio in it. What a grand idea Ray thought as the radio would keep him abreast of the activity of the cops which would clearly allow him to not be in the same vicinity they were in. Could he pull this off without a weapon? He had to give it a shot. It meant his freedom at every level. Jake Simpson was the custodian at the parking garage of the Police station. Drive there and make like he was about to park his car there . When Jake opened the door Ray would pick something small, easy on gas and efficient enough to get him where he needed to be. It was going according to plan as Jake who was about to retire came out to see who had just parked in his lot.

"Can I help you?" Jake called out. Ray did not answer but kept walking up to Jake. Jake was holding the door open to see if he knew this person parking here. His eyes opened wide as he recognized the face of Sgt Ray Blue.

"How could this be? You died in that awful plane crash." Jake stammered out but Ray pushed him in the shop then turning back to the door locked it.

"I need a new car. What have you got?" Ray mentioned.

"I just can't allow you to come in here and demand a new car. These cars are for active Police Officers. I suggest you better leave or it will be too bad for you." Jake did not believe Ray would hurt a fellow officer but he was wrong. Picking up the model knife Jake had gotten from his son on his birthday which Jake displayed openly on his desk, Ray stabbed him twice in the belly. As Jake fell to the floor, Ray looked at the listings of cars which hung on the wall. There was a small four door car just brought in by a female officer so Ray seeing where the keys were went to the large box which hung on the wall opening it to see the keys were hung with the letterings of the area the cars were parked in. taking the keys Ray left the door for the keys open but looked down at old Jake. He was still alive so Ray took the gift knife and stabbed him repeatedly then put the knife in his pocket. Jake was a cop but was forbidden to possess a gun which was well known with all the cops. So leaving the shop Ray went down the driveway until he came across the car he was after.

The doors were locked so using the keys Ray unlocked the door of the driver's side then got in. Starting it up right away he backed it up then turning the steering wheel to the left, he pulled away. There on his right of the console was a small police radio which Ray was glad to see. Now he could go visit the bait shop to get what he needed to go against the Unholy Ones. Heading out of town through the back streets kept Ray alert of any opportunity of seeing bikers or activities of bikers. Yes he knew of the many drug dealers in these areas which was a good way of keeping track of where these fuckers might be. Finally he had reached the bait shop. Noticing the open sign on the door Ray parked his car just to the left of the front entrance between two other cars parked there. Turning off the engine Ray sat in the car for a moment debating with himself if he should take a couple of painkillers before going in. The pain in his left side was excruciating but he knew he had to keep his senses until he was fully equipped with the weapons he needed to make his move on the bikers. This pain was a fond experience of why he hated them even more than what they did to his wife or Sherry and of course his son. Slamming his fist against the steering wheel he thought of his son. The child was alive somewhere so he had to find him and still build a relationship. Until that time came, Ray needed to finish what he first set out to do. Opening the car door Ray slid out of the car. Every move he made sent a shot of pain through him so now was the time to get this done. He had to go around to the front of the bait shop to go up the stairs because there was no side door just the one front door. There was no window to peer in so he could see if there were others shopping in there but be it as it may, it was a well-known place for hunters and fishermen to shop for the tools of their trade. Turning the knob to open the door, a little bell rang giving evidence someone had entered the shop. Looking around Ray saw three other people inside so he made his way to the front counter.

"Yes, good afternoon sir, may I help you?" Came a voice from behind him. It was someone showing another customer some product he was interested in buying. Ray did not turn around to see where the person was but waited at the counter for the person to come to him.

Yes sir. I am sorry about that may I help you?" It was a guy about thirty years old and had a tinge of Charlie's looks, maybe his son.

"Yes hello." Ray started. " Is Charlie around?"

"I'm sorry but my father passed away last year. May I be of assistance?"

"I'm sorry to hear that. Well I am looking for something in a Smith & Weston, maybe a Magnum." Ray began.

"Well I can certainly help you with that. Do you have any particular size?"

"Would you happen to have on hand a .44 Magnum or a .357?"

"I do have both but they are certainly not the same." Opening a glass display case the young man brought out the .44 Magnum watching Ray handle it.

"This gun suits you if you don't mind me saying." Ray agreed with him He like the feel of it in his hand and knew the damage it could cause if anyone got hit from a shot from it.

"How much is it?" Ray asked. He did not want to go overboard with the spending knowing full well he had enough cash to make it a sale.

"This particular piece is on sale from four fifty to three fifty. We usually have a sale around this time of year to attract gun users like yourself."

"Then I'll take it. How much are the cartledges?"

"How much is the ammo?" Ray asked again.

"Well a twelve pack is $50.00 and the 24 pack is $ 90.00"

"Ok then I will take 10 of the 24 packs." Ray wanted to make sure he had enough to go all around. " Also do you carry the Glock?"

"Yes but we would have to order that certain brand. Would you like me to put in an order?"

Ray thought about it a moment then told him.

"No this should suffice."

"Ok then. All that is needed is for some identification."

Ray hauled out his identification and with it he showed his badge which was enough for the young man.

"Oh you are a Police Officer well that changes things." Ray was stunned.

"What do you mean?"

"Well Police Officers get an additional fifteen percent discount." Ray was able to breathe again. He would have loaded the gun and shot this guy if he had said he could not get it.

"Oh one other thing." Ray reminded himself so he had to get one. " I need a holster, preferably over the shoulder." The young man went into the back to get the holster ray had asked for. Coming back he helped Ray put it on then Ray placed the loaded gun in the holster. Taking out his wife's Mastercard he usually carried because she liked to shop he gave it to the young man who ran it through the machine which came back as a good card. Why use up all his cash if the plastic worked. It was in Claire's name so the bill would show up in her name. But Ray knew he would never return to the address he once lived at. He did though have a camp in Tennessee he could stay at if need be. It was out in the Ozarks hidden from anyone who would be out there. Who would venture out that far was not in their right mind so Ray had a second place to stay after he was finished with the bikers for good. Feeling a lot better because he felt naked not having a gun Ray returned to the car. Getting in he started it up but before putting the car into gear he turned on the radio to see if there was any news about the bikers.

"Let's see what we got," Ray said to himself, " one-zero-one." Within a minute a call went out.

"One-zero-one calling."

"This one twenty three. What's up one-zero-one?"

"You are to check out a disturbance at the county line. People have been calling in about a bunch of bikers calling themselves the Unholy Ones. Use extreme caution they may be armed and dangerous. you need back up call for it."

"Roger one-zero-one I'm on my way."

"Remember to call for back up one twenty three we don't need dead heroes." The cops were on their way with lights flashing but no siren. They did not want to frighten these bikers off. Ray on the otherhand knew the area well so he began his trek over that way a little better prepared with his new weapon. Going down the main road to the county line Ray saw up ahead the cops turn towards the county line road. It was a road seldom used anymore since they brought in the highway so these bikers used roads like this to evade from capture. It was used by the Federal boys chasing down Moonshiners in the day. Ray kept a good distance away from the cop car up ahead of him not wanting to tip his hand he saw where they were headed. It was the old Mccurty homestead. Yeah it was abandoned but a good place to hole up if it became a need. There was an outhouse in the back. It had a pump in the front yard for clean water and even if there were a few rats running through the house one could have a sleep without any problems. Parking his car off the road hidden by trees and bushes like before, Ray continued on foot with his gun in his hand and the safety off. Even getting shot in the gut was enough to cut someone in half.

Ray did not care just as long it was one of those fucking bikers or even the girls who enjoyed getting fucked up the ass then sucking them off. They all deserved death. The world would breathe a lot easier with them gone forever. Getting closer to the old farm Ray heard familiar voices. These were the ones who left him for dead. Ray became very cautious because he did not need another beating. Suddenly he stopped in his tracks as the noise became louder. The cops did not pay attention to their superiors figuring they could handle the situation themselves by becoming cowboys. The bikers had a different idea. They were told not to take an unnecessary chance but to call for back up because they did not pay attention they were now prisoners of the bikers who cared less if they died. It did not bother Ray if they died. He only cared about killing the bikers, all of them.

Creeping into the camp via the wooded area Ray had passed the whole lot of them. As he passed by he counted well over sixty of them together huddled into one big mass. Ray wished he still had the C-4 to wake them up pronto but all he had was a gun that held six bullets at a time. Yes they were very deadly bullets but he had to keep reloading. If he could somehow manage to get the ring leaders then the rest would be left in a confusion then taking them down one at a time would be so much easier. So Ray's sights were for Crazy, Fixer and Coaster.

"Crazy?" One of the bikers coming back from the woods after having a whiz thought he saw Ray but wasn't too sure.

"What is it?" C razy answered. He looked a little pissed off for some reason maybe it was the idea the cops knew where they were holed up.

"I thought I saw the cop we beat at the other place where the pit was." He mentioned not too sure of himself. Ray heard it as well so he lay down under some underbrush incase they came searching the area for him.

"Whadda ya mean you saw him. What was it his ghost? We killed that motherfucker back at the pit. So forget about him we got us a couple more cops to deal with. One of them looks like he's too young to shave. I got an idea bring the whores over here." As the biker rounded up the whores they came with him to see what Crazy was up to.

"okay girls take his clothes off him completely." The young cop tried to fight the girls off but received a couple shots in the head while the girls tore his uniform off him. Once he was naked infront of everyone the other cop looked around for a chance to get away. Pushing the biker away from him he made a beeline into the woods to get away. Crazy looked up watching the cop make it for the woods then he barked out some orders.

"Flattoe you and Kicker take care of that cop. He can't get away. If he gets back to his station or makes a call the place will be flooding with cops." The two bikers chased after the cop. They were younger and in better shape which helped them catch the cop who put up a good fight but did not fare too well against the bikers. They stabbed him numerous times before leaving him where he was then started to return to the fold. But they met someone that wasn't afraid of them, no he was happy to meet the two of them here in the woods. Taking out the knife he had in his pocket, Ray stabbed one so hard he almost broke the biker's ribs. The other one tried to free his friend but ended up getting stabbed to death as well. Ray wanted them all dead so he returned to watch what they had planned for the young cop. Apparently a biker by the name of Pickles was queer. When he saw the young cop's dick he started salivating to have it bounce around in his mouth. Crazy did not like queers but since he was Fixer's younger brother he had to allow him access to the bike group. Crazy saw Pickles crave to be with the cop so he called out to him.

"Pickles I want you to take him up the ass dry. If you want to taste him by all means, go ahead." Pickles did not have to be told twice. He pounced on the young cop turning him over so the cop was face first to the ground he dropped his jeans driving his hard cock up the cop's tight, dry ass. The young cop cried out in pain and the more he cried the more the whores and bikers laughed cheering Pickles on to finish the job. Finally Pickles exploded in the young cop and wanted to do him again, looking at Crazy for permission, Crazy told him.

"Go ahead he's all yours." Everyone laughed at the way Pickles was fucking this poor soul who wished he had listened to his superior not to approach without back-up. Ray did not care for the cop taking it up the ass. The young cop did not listen to his instructions so he deserved whatever happened to him. Crazy then lifted his head in the air wondering where Flattoe and Kicker were.

"Has anyone seen Flattoe or Kicker since they went after that cop?" No one was paying attention to Crazy as they were finding humor in Pickles screwing the shit out of the young cop. Crazy asked again with a louder voice.

"Listen up fuckheads." When he had the attention of all of them again he asked. " Has anyone seen Flattoe or Kicker since they went after that cop?" No one answered which got Crazy to talk again.

"Me either. Fixer take a couple of whores and go search the woods for them. We cannot afford those cops to know we are here, when you find them and they are alright bring them here to me."

"What time is it?" Freddie "Fixer" Burgess asked as he was not in the mood to go after two renegade bikers. Fixer liked to sleep through the day and rouse about at night.

"It's seven-thirty bother." Pickles told his big brother Fixer. " Now you are up will you tell these girls to stop teasing me."

"Yeah, yeah when I wake up, now fuck off. Go find yourself a stray dog but make sure it's a male or you could end up straight." Everyone roared at what Fixer had said to his queer brother. You know, they should have listened to the fairy because Ray figured it was time to take care of them when Fixer and two girls left the camp insearch for the two missing bikers. Moving a breath away from the camp Ray took aim shooting he squeezed off a shot hitting Rigger in the left eye which blew the back of his head off. The girls screamed in fear as Crazy went for his gun but he wasn't fast enough as Ray let another shot go off hitting Crazy right in the crotch. Reeling around on the ground Crazy held his crotch as the intense pain shot through him. Ray did not have to worry about him for awhile as he had to take care of a couple more heavyweights before cleaning out this nest of vipers. Fixer came running back to the camp to see his brother Rigger laying on the ground with only half of a head. Looking to his right he saw Crazy holding his balls as blood spurted everywhere. Turning to the woods Fixer was trying to get a bead on the one firin g at the bikers so running towards the woods he scooped up Crazy's gun and began firing it wildly hoping he would hit the one causing dissention in the camp. Big mistake. If he had taken his time to train the gun at the spot he probably would have killed Ray but Fixer's shots were not even close as Ray stood up stepping into a clearing it was too late for Fixer as he saw Ray. He tried to brithe gun around to kill the cop but Ray beat him to the draw, firing again Fixer took the bullet in the chest making Fixer fly off his feet onto his back. Ray eyeballed the whole camp to see who was left. Not too many as the rest jumped on their bikes and roared out of the area. Ray took his time coming into the camp as he did not want any unwanted surprises coming at him. Ray did not care about the girls they were on their own now. He wanted the coward who pissed his pants and was hiding behind Pickles. Of course it was Crazy. Pickles was wounded in the right leg from a shot his brother Fixer had done when he first started shooting blindly.

"So your name is Pickles eh? How did you ever get a name like that?"

"Because I like male pickles." The queer admitted. " Would you like yours massaged?"

"Shut the fuck up or I'll make sure you die a slow, agonizing death." Ray looked at him asking, you love cock do you? Well maybe you were meant to be a woman. Ray need a piss so he hauled out his cock pissing all over the queer. Then putting it back in his pants he grabbed a hold of the queer telling him to drop his jeans.

"I want you to drop your jeans down." The queer was all for it so standing up which was hard because of the bullet he had in his leg he overcame the pain to stand before Ray unfastening his pants letting them fall to his ankles. Ray reached out grabbing his cock and in one movement cut the queers cock off. Pickles fell on his back in shock as blood squirted everywhere. Then looking down at Crazy he asked him,

"Where is my son?" Crazy smiled up at him telling him, " somewhere safe."

"Listen you better tell me or I will end it right now for you." Crazy knew if he talked it ewasn't going to change things. He would die no matter what. So to cause more grief to the cop he told him to go fuck himself. Thoughts of being in Cambodia during the war in Nam filled his mind. It was from the death camp the North Vietnamese used in Cambodia for disillusioned young warriors just in from the States who thought they could make a difference. These kids did not know what they were getting into. They were never told the horrors that were happening over there but the ones that came back did. That was the big reason there were riots across the States to end the war. American pilots were just as bad dropping napalm on their own armies. The kids were told to kill, yes kill the ones oppressing the free world. Some free world. That is why many never got the chance to grow up in a normal world being sent straight to Saigon. And these motherfucking bikers were probably draft dodgers. Well whatever they were, they started a war they could never win. The person who became their enemy was a medal winning Green Beret.

Never was there ever anyone as qualified as their foe than Ray. These bikers were nothing but cowards because they could not give their opponent a fair shake. If they did it would be the end of them. They also enjoyed picking on the elderly and children. Nothing more than child molesting bastards. Telling these kids they loved them and their love was endless. Sure they would get lots of loving but not in the way these children imagined. The young girls had to fuck all the bikers who wanted to taste the wares of these kids. In normal life these motherfuckers could never have a solid relationship with a woman, it was just something they knew nothing about. But to steal a child away from her parents was the conquest they had to justify their evil plans. As Ray thought of what they did to these innocent, wholesome girls it made him not only sick but crazier in his efforts to wipe them all out. Ray looked at the queer asking him straight forward questions.

"Go to hell." Pickles answered which enraged Ray. Going to the camp fire Ray picked out a red hot stick with burning embers on it. " One more chance. Here's the main clubhouse?"

Pickles said nothing so Ray stuck the red hot stick into his crotch to not only stop what little bleeding there was left but to cauterize the area.

"AWWWRRGH! You fucking cop. Go to hell. You want to know where the clubhouse is? Then go find it."

Ray thought of killing him as what use would he be but if he let him linger on suffering as much pain as possible maybe he could play a larger part in the strategy he was thinking of.

Going back to the fire Ray hauled another burning stick out then turning to face Pickles, he laughed as he stuck it in the hole Ray had made when he cut Pickle's little cock off which made the queer pass out from the pain. Grabbing him by the collar Ray dragged him to his car. As he was going to his car he saw the young cop. Still alive with a bloody ass and in extreme pain caused by his own disobedience of the chain of command. When he got back to the car he popped the trunk maneuvering Pickles inside then closed the door. This was going to be larger than ray first realized. One good thing was in this area he could go to the local law agency without detection and give them Pickles. But first he had to finish what he came here to do. Crazy who sheltered himself behind the queer had now used a young girl who had been shot in the gut. She was trying to cling on but was failing at her mission. Ray did not care about her.

He wanted Crazy for his own. Then Ray surmised, why waste ammo when there were other good ways of putting him down. Picking up a burning stick he walked over to Crazy asking as he approached.

"You get one chance let me know what I want to know and you can go on living fuck with me and you will die a painful death."

"Go fuck yourself cop. I have nothing to say to you." Ray looked at him smiling then told him.

"I kind of knew this was what you were going to say so I have a real treat for you." Crazy stared at him with his eyes wide open as Ray took the red hot stick driving it into his throat. More blood shot from Crazy as Ray sat there watching him bleed to death. Unlike Crazy, Ray was not going to leave until he knew he was dead. It did not take long as Crazy's eyes began to glaze over. The young girl reached out to Ray for help but he kicked her hand away.

"Who was it that wanted me dead? Well looks like the shoe is on the other foot. Suffer and die." He left the camp heading down highway forty-one to a law enforcement office he knew about. The Sheriff there wasn't the brightest so Ray would drop Pickles off as a gift then continue on his trek. The Police station was just off the highway so pulling into the driveway Ray looked at the building walked in and met a cute older receptionist.

"Good day, I'd like to see the Sheriff he is in." Ray asked.

"Sure you go to the door at the end of the hall that's his office." She answered smiling.

": Thank you." Turning to his left he walked along the corridor until he came to the end. Rapping on the door brought an answer from behind the door.

"Come in." Ray saw a pudgy older man sitting behind a desk so he walked in letting him know why he was here.

"Hello. I was told you are the one in command here."

"You were told right mister. Come in and let me know how I can assist you."

"Well I was down at the old county line and I heard shots so I took the opportunity to pull over on the side of the road when I heard someone getting shot. I did not want to stick around just incase I might get killed for being a witness so I high-tailed it out of there straight here as fast I could to let you know."

"Well it was smart of you to leave this mess in the hands of the Police. What's your name Partner?"

"Roger Smith." Ray lied. He did not want it known he were still alive.

"Well Roger I wouldn't be too alarmed. Probably some kids having some fun. I'll send a couple of Deputies to check it out. But could I get your address and phone number incase we need to get in touch with you." Ray gave a phony address along with a cell phone number his wife used to have. It was all he could think of at the moment not realizing they would ask for those items. God he was a cop did he not think of this stupid part of trying to get support from a sheriff's office. Leaving He overheard the sheriff talk with a couple of his deputies.

"Now it has been over nine hours since Officer Brown and Tingley went to check on that disturbance over at the county line and now this fellow wanders in here saying he heard shots fired over there. Have any of you heard from them?" He asked his deputies who just stood there shaking their heads no. Then he went on. " I believe there might be some foul play there so I suggest all of go and investigate to make sure our guys are safe and sound." They left in a hurry as Ray witnessed them jump into their cars speeding towards the old county line road. It was getting dark so when the deputies and the sheriff arrived it took them a little longer to get their eyes accustomed to the darkness. Yes the squad car was there but no officers to be seen. The sheriff shone his searchlight on the area and was taken aback from the dead bodies lying infront of him. The two deputies with flashlights in one of their hands, while their guns were in the other searched the area. They could not believe their eyes when they found their ftellow officer laying on the ground with his pants down to his ankles and his ass covered in shit and blood. The decent thing they could do was to get an ambulance out here to rush him to the hospital. Also they called the "meat wagon," to take care of the young girls and dead bikers. Something was certainly amiss here as the Sheriff surmised someone other than the bikers came her and killed all these people. Ray on the otherhand was still in the parking lot of the sheriff and wanted to leave quickly because the sheriff would be pissed if he realized he had a renegade cop in his clutches especially one who was supposed to have died in an air disaster. Picking up speed on the highway Ray wanted the sheriff's department to be as far away as possible. Ray figured the sheriff would be smart enough to call in the State Troopers and to ray he thought very little about that let them deal with that mess. He had other plans which needed to be looked over. Finding the clubhouse was a major concern to Ray because there would be a couple hundred of the bastards partying together. A great opportunity for Ray to blow them all the fuck up. Ray knew the Sheriff and the deputies would come to the understanding Ray had something to do with the crash but right now they could not put their finger on it so this was the reason the sheriff called in the State Troopers who would take a description of the fellow reporting the mess at the county line road telling the sheriff this fellow was a Sargeant on the force next door and was wanted for questioning in the air disaster where one hundred and fourteen people lost their lives. Ray had to be super careful now so he would not be recognized. He did not want to lose out giving those bastards a taste of their own treatments. Their reward as Ray saw it.

Travelling on the back roads and off the highway just incase the State Troopers put out a bulletin on Ray as a dangerous loose cannon. It really helped to have the foresight to grab a car with a two-way radio.

Up ahead on a country road were some really weird freaks a whole congregation of krishna's with their hands out for passing cars to get a donation from them. Behind them were what seemed about ten bikers. He had to come to a slow pace with his car so he would not hit anyone as he tried to maneuver his car around these freaks they just would not move out of the way.

"May the Lord be with you." They chanted as they tried to get some poor sucker to throw them some cash.

"You want cash? I'll give you cash." Ray roared at them as he revved the engine veering into the crowd. Taking about three of them with him ray did not care just as long as he could take out those ten bikers. Keeping his foot on the gas until those clinging on the car lost their lives by his careless driving.

"Hare Krishna that mother fucker." Ray blurted out laughing at them for the foolish way they lived their lives.

As Ray came over the next rise on the country highway he stopped suddenly. Lying out there before him was his quarry. Zooming down right after them, he cared little if there were radar set-up points which he doubted were there because now these assholes had to contend with the State Troopers and if they knew these bikers were here then there would be a force of State Troopers visiting them. But because Ray had to run down the Krishnas someone in their numbers called the Police and complained.

"Arrrrrr." Sirens blew as Ray checked his rear-view mirror he saw two squad cars coming up fast on his ass. Slowing down he came to a complete stop. The cars proved to be State Troopers which pulled up behind him. Coming up to the driver's side and passengers the Troopers had their guns out ready to fire if need be.

"Good afternoon officer." Ray started. " I am sorry if I gave the impression that I was late for a job interview but one of those bikers down there is not really a biker. I have been trailing him for some time now. He's a cop who is wanted for questioning in a murder that happened over Carleston. Now I know there's a reward for anyone leading to his arrest and I aim on getting that." The Trooper did not buy his story but repeated his command.

"Sir get out of the car now. Put your hands on your head and get down on your knees."

"Sure." Ray answered as he opened the door to get out. He dropped to his knees firing off a shot taking the cop standing not ten feet away in the forehead. The Trooper fell backwards dead before he hit the pavement. The other cop nervous because was never in a situation like this before fired randomly in the direction of Ray but his shots ran wild. When his gun was empty he tried to reload but never had the chance as Ray shot him and killed him as well. This was not the end as two more Trooper cars were coming after him as well so jumping back in the car Ray started it up but decided not to run. Turning the car off he hid on the passenger side until the Troopers had reached the site gotten out of their vehicles as ray waited for them to become clearer victims.

"Jesus look at this mess. We better call the Sheriff and let him know what we have on our hands." Then one of the Troopers walked towards the bushes guarding the road as his partner called in the report then getting out of the car he asked his partner what he was up to. Before the other Trooper could answer his partner understood where he was up to as he pissed beside Ray's car. Ray hauled out his knife as he had a trick he used many times on the Vietcong to bring them down. As he was about to make his move the other Trooper called out to him. " Javen where the fuck did you go? C'mon we have a ton of paperwork to do so hurry up and get your ass out here." Waiting another five minutes he went on the search for his partner. Not finding him he even called out his name several times, no answer. It was going to be a long night for Jack Wallace as his younger brother was not to be found. Jack was becoming sick as he knew the renegade cop was close by so instead of continuing the search he got in his car backing up to turn around he ran over a heavy bump which he never did when he had arrived so putting the car into park he jumped out to see what he had ran over. Laying right there under the car now was his younger brother. Jack pulled his brother out not wanting to run over him again seeing his throat was slashed. Jack was scared so when he stood up he hauled out his gun then thought it best to just get in the car and return to the Sheriff's office. As he got in Ray was sitting inside waiting for the helpless cop who had put his gun away before getting into the car. Ray's slash ended the Trooper's life just like Javen. Before the blood shot all over the inside of the car Ray pushed him to the pavement then coming over to the driver's side he took the Troopers car instead. It was an interceptor. A lot faster better handling. Ray took off this highway heading west instead of east meaning he took the wrong road. He had to be on double duty watching the skies as well because he fucked with the Sheriff's department and they would no doubt get the choppers out. Funny they would not do this for him when his wife was taken, Ray thought to himself. On the old road he was on he came to a fork on the road. Ray had to think which way would be more beneficial to him, taking the right side, which he realized was a terrible mistake as it had him heading west instead of east because the road wound back around like a snake. The whir of a chopper told him what he had suspected about the Sheriff's department. Ray did not drive instead he parked near some heavy area of trees which kept him well hidden. Getting out of the car was good for him as he could stretch his legs and have an overdue piss which really felt good. Going back to the car he wished he had the fore thought of bringing a bottle of water he left in the other car. He had to grin and bear it for the time being. Looking at the side of the Trooper's car it read Supervisor. So going back to the inside of the car he took the keys out of the ignition then came to the back of the car opening the trunk. " My god." Was Ray's expression as he could not believe his eyes. It was a storehouse of weapons. Two oozies sat there with enough ammo to fill them three or four times, a small crate with twelve grenades and a twelve gauge pump. Taking out the shotgun Ray checked to see if the gun was loaded, " locked and loaded," was the term he used when checking his ammo over in Nam. Sitting on the edge of the trunk Ray pulled out the smokes he found in the car after he took it. Apparently the Trooper smoked. He always heard it was a good way to suppress hunger and he was hungry so taking a smoke out of the pack he placed it between his lips then realized he had nothing to light it with so again taking the keys out of the trunk lock to the ignition he half turned the ignition, not to start the car but to get the lighter which just above the ashtray then pushing it in he waited about ten seconds when it popped out with a red glow telling him it was hot enough to light his cigarette which he did. At first inhaling was hard as his lungs were not used to the gray smoke filling them so he started coughing. The more he inhaled the better it was for his body to adjust to the smoke filling his lungs. What he was told about the suppression of hunger was true. So when that smoke was finished he lit up another one. Now ray smoked cigarettes and why not? What did he have to lose? He lost everything else so if he died from smoking what was the big deal. Shaking those thoughts out of his head, he had to come up with what was happening right now. Again the chopper passed overhead getting Ray to duck down even though he could not be seen. It was just a reflex of the past came into play. Taking the oozies out of the trunk with all the clips he placed them on the floor just before the front passenger seat. Any fast driving with a twist and turn could be disasterous if they were on the seat falling to the floor then going off as he drove could cost him his life, not yet, he cared little if he died but he certainly did not come this far to have it end quite right now. No he wanted to end the existence of the unholy ones once and for all. Then if for some reason other cops put him away they so be it. Before starting the car up he thought to himself when he looked at the fire power in his possession, " Come on now you fucking cowards. Let's see your balls now." Swearing a few obscenities to himself but as his eyes caught his face in the rear-view mirror he saw he had his cold grin back. This had to be the final battle for his wife, babysitter and his son. But not only them. How many officers had to give their lives up because of all this bullshit? Everyone these animals had ruined. The families they broke up and leaving young ones without parents. They say pay back is a bitch well whoever said those words knew what they were talking about.

CHAPTER VII

Ray pulled deep into the woods so no one could see him if they somehow found this road to travel. Getting out of the car he went over to a pile of fallen pine limbs which he thought would be a good place to lie down. Stretching out on them it wasn't long before he was snoozing. It had been two days since he got the needed rest to be on top of the game alert and wise. Without sleep he would fuck up on the strategic decisions so this was his opportunity to take advantage of the time needed. This sleep carried him until the morning of the next day because the silence made it so peaceful. Waking up it took him a few minutes to remember where he was and why he was here. When all the shit from the last few weeks hit him, he sat up with a growling stomach. He was really hungry. When he was totally up he stretched and went behind a tree to have a nice long piss. It really felt good but through the night he caught a chill which he tried to shake off knowing it came from not eating. Going over to the car he reached into the glove compartment to retrieve the smokes he put in there and found a large bar of chocolate. Opening it slowly Ray salivated for the sweetness to melt in his mouth. He knew he had to eat it slow or he would get stomach cramps and he did not want them, what he needed most of all was a tall glass of cold water. This chocolate bar was not the best breakfast he ever had but then again it wasn't the worse. It was something to take the gnawing pain out of his gut until he had sustenance in a more healthier way.

Ray remembered when he was in Cambodia when he only had crickets to eat or starve. He ate the crickets but thought of the fried chicken his mother used to prepare for him. He could still taste the fried chicken she served and the more he remembered the more he yearned so he thought of something else. Going behind the car Ray gathered some small twigs and branches to make a smoke free fire. He had to warm himself up, as the fire began to take he held his hands over the fire then rubbed them over his body. It felt really good he thought about this but what pissed him off the most to get the fire going he had to use the lighter above the ashtray in the car. Walking up the road when he was satisfied his body was beginning to respond to the heat he supplied, he found a trickle of cold spring water. Bending down he cupped his hands taking three or four handfuls of the cold water. After he straightened up did he start getting the cramps. Rubbing his belly it seemed to help get rid of the cramps when he started farting. One big, long, stinky fart came out which made him think he lost five pounds with that one but it sure felt good. Now he was ready to go back to the car light up a smoke and get the hell out of here. Sitting in the car Ray again farted so bad he had to get out of the car until it aired out. Once he was comfortable in the car Ray started it up then moved along the small road. To his surprise it took him to the highway which he pulled out on making sure there was no cars coming his way. Speeding up Ray had to make up for lost time so he was careless as he sped up the highway reaching ninety miles an hour right past a Sheriff's Deputy car waiting for some sucker who thought he could drive like a maniac. Pulling out behind Ray the lights were flashing as the Deputy gave chase. Within a moment the siren was screetching which Ray did not want to happen so reaching over to the passenger seat he fit the pistol into his hand then slowed down pulling over to the side of the road but to Ray's astonishment the Sheriff's car went past him as if he were called to something more important. Ray smelled something burning from his engine so getting out of the car he saw he needed a pint of oil. He was alright for now but soon he needed to make sure the car was remedied if he wanted to keep the interceptor as his own. Getting back into the car Ray started checking the dials on his radio but there was a dead silence. He could not see why because of the Deputy racing past him.

Yesterday orders issued out for the ones on the road but today it was weird not to know what was going on. Frustrated with the cop radio he turned it off turning on the regular radio checking all the stations until he found a good country station listening for awhile he again became bored so turning this radio off he tried the to-way again. Nothing came in so not really watching what he was doing Ray turned both radioes on at the same time. That was the combination needed to get a report from the Sheriff's office. Smooth, real smooth thinking as the operator of this vehicle had a brain to set the radio up like this. It wasn't a perfect combination though or Ray would never been able to find the right one to listen in.

"Anyone with their ears on, come back, anyone with their ears on, come back."

"This is car thirty-three. What's on your mind?"

"Car thirty-three check out the county line back road. There's reports of a small fire could be our man."

"Done, thirty-three out."

Ray was glad he had left the area when he did. He must have forgot to put out the small fire he started to get warm. The another call came over the two-way.

"Thirty-three come back?"

"This is thirty-three what's up?"

"Thirty-three there's sightings of the bikers at Middle Creek. Go check it out only. I repeat check it out only. Proceed with caution they may be armed and dangerous. We just need a confirmation, do you copy?"

"Yes I copy over and out." There was no way the Deputy was going to let this golden opportunity pass through his fingers. If he could bring down the lead biker he would get a much needed promotion. So off he went to check out Middle Creek

Ray was also on his way to Middle Creek as soon as he found it on the road map lodged in the cubbie hole on the door. Ray peeled from his position on the side of the road looking at the speedometer he saw he was going one hundred and fifty miles an hour yet he didn't have it to the boards. Whatever was in this car, well, it sure worked. Then Ray remembered the oil situation and started slowing down. He did not need to blow the engine then where would he be? There was a truck stop just ahead on the right with a gas station so Ray took the opportunity to go get some gas and get the oils situation taken care of. As he pulled up to the pumps a pretty young girl came out to service him.

"Good morning may I help you?" She asked smiling down at Ray who decided to get out of the car and pop the hood.

"Yeah would you fill her up with premium." Then reaching into the engine to pull out the rod to tell him his oil dilemma he asked the girl.

"You got any ten-forty oil?"

"Yes sir right over there." She answered pointing to the pile of oils cans sitting on a shelf. Going over Ray opened the oil tray then opened the can pouring the oil in the car he let all of it pour into the car. Then closing the hood he went back to the car to sit behind the wheel as the young girl came to the window telling him,

"That'll be forty dollars even for the gas and can of oil." Ray hauled out of his pocket the wad of money he had passing her a fifty he told her. " Keep the change." They back on the road he cared little about eating right now he had to get to Middle Creek before the young Deputy. Up ahead was an overpass which was a marker he was getting close to Middle Creek. The young Deputy was driving around eighty miles an hour but not fast enough as Ray blew past him. He was purposely letting this young Deputy know what it was like to face a real enemy. It was not 5the cardboard copies they had to teach their Deputies at the Academy, no it was real fuckers who'd shoot you dead just because they needed to prove to the public what tough boys they were. Deep down Ray knew what they were, nothing but scuzzbags who needed to be beaten to death each and every one of them. Aw, Ray wanted to make them suffer the same indignities he had to suffer. That his loving, kind wife had to suffer, that his babysitter and her family had to suffer and finally his son. Didn't he have the right to know who his real parents were. The more Ray thought about it the more he remembered how he used to stalk his enemies in the jungles. It was happening again like some sort of bad dream. They say history has a way of repeating itself but that war ended and this one was about to end. He came out of the first one without being injured physically but mentally he was fucked up like so many more returning from the war. Like being on an extended vacation, Ray was ready for action.

After a long wait the Deputy's car was swallowed up by the forest. Ray had waited patiently knowing the Deputy would take longer as he was younger and inexperienced but as soon as Ray caught a glimpse of the squad car coming his way he stayed where he was in the car behind some bushes so when the Deputy passed him then Ray got out of his vehicle with all the ammo he could carry. The trek through the forest was challenging with him carrying the hardware with its ammo. Not knowing just how far he had to go was something he wondered about as well. Always on the alert as some biker could still be watching the road even if the Deputy came through. Ray heard the cries and music of the bikers. There were quite a few here as it was a Jamboree meaning all the boy scouts were here. Ray now realized he was in the midst of his enemies yet, he was undetected, Going off the road Ray saw a large spruce tree on his right so going over to it he sat under the branches waiting for the darkness to envelope the land. Ray always did his dirty work in the night. It gave him better shelter when he was going up against extra amounts of odds. Crash went some branches on a tree not ten yards away from him. It was some hapless biker with something more than fighting on his mind. With him was a young girl who looked like she couldn't have been more than fourteen years old which he figured he would have as she was new pussy brought back to the camp today. The biker came right up to Ray who he never saw and started pissing on him. Ray swore he would cut his nuts off, feed them to him and as Ray made a move to get him but thought it would be better under the cover of darkness. Darkness was Ray's friend in the past especially when he was overseas and now he needed it to be his friend. Drawing his mind off of what was taking place right now he kept going over in his mind what his plan was and why he was here. When he heard the young girl cry out thoughts of Ray's family came to mind. These had to be pushed out of his mind or they would allow for mistakes to happen which would end his life. The biker began walking around making a terrible noise not caring about anything except getting back to the fold, too bad, Ray just could not wait any longer he had no patience for waiting, just like being put on hold on a phone, Ray would just hang up. Springing forward Ray caught the biker by the throat he moved his hand to the top of the head as he looked precariously around the forest to see if this guy was alone, seeing there was no one else with his right hand Ray pulled out his knife slitting the biker's throat then as a precaution buried him under a tree. It was a good place for him as this tree was also a spruce tree where Ray had been staying. Going over to see the young girl he just raped, it turned his stomach to see the blood everywhere as the dead body of such a precious little girl abused by a sadistic piece of shit just lay there lifeless. It really hit home with Ray as he sat there starting to cry because how many young girls were put into a situation of demoralizing sexual acts so these bikers could get their jollies then leave them dead. What about these young girl's parents how did they feel not ever seeing their little ones ever again or not knowing what ever happened to them. Looking at her, tears poured down his face because he had gone through a trauma with the death of his wife, his babysitter and heaven's knows where his son was. Would his son ever get to know the truth of who his real father was or even who his loving mother was? Ray tried to stand by pushing himself up. His strength for going on was beginning to wane

As Ray had gone back to the spruce tree one more time to get his automatic rifles the ammo and the powerful handgun he had under his belt with extra ammo. When he had made his mind up to attack he was disrupted by the whine of sirens with about fifteen Sheriff's cars rushing into the camp to free their young co-worker the Deputy who came here late in the day to show these bikers they were dealing with someone who was not afraid. Jumping out of their carts with guns blazing the Deputies cared little if there were other hostages there, too bad for them, all the Deputies wanted was to free their friend taking him back safely. When they entered the camp which was one of ten other camps the bikers made incase something like this happened, they saw their friend nailed to a tree naked. There was evidence the bikers played with him through torture with the many marks across his body. Even to the point of being castrated as blood was evident all over his legs. One thing these Deputies never figured out was these bikers were sworn killers not even caring for the young girls they expropriated from loving, caring families. No, They would use these young girls as a diversion to ward off the Police. Ray sat there watching the whole melee from the beginning to the end when the bikers verged on the Deputies from all sides to make sure there was minimal damage to the biker family. The bikers would make damn sure there were no survivors from the threat that visited their camp uninvited. When it was over Ray stood above the camp looking down on about forty bikers congregated together dealing with what just happened and how to deal with it again if something like this were to take place. Ray saw they were dazed from this mess that just happened so he took advantage of it. When Ray got down into the camp undetected he remembered he had a small chunk of C-4 in his jacket pocket so taking it out he placed certain pieces around the bikes. He only needed to set off two or three pieces because when the bikes exploded it would become a domino affect setting off the other bikes. Then instead of making it obvious he changed his mind to place a small piece to the spark plugs of the bikes which would have immediate reactions blowing the bikes to kingdom come. After the bikes had been toyed with he waited for the bikers to come back to the huddle in the camp with the young girls, Ray could not hold back any longer as he jumped up firing both automatic rifles taking quite a few of them with the first volley of fire. Ducking down he tried to get in a position which would really cripple these fuckers. Again he stood firing at them as they scurried like rats for cover, he fired and fired until his chambers were empty then as quick as he could slipped another clip into each gun. This was better than Ray thought it would be. Many of the bikers lay dead on the forest floor and yes there were plenty of girls dead as well but this was the price of messing with Ray. As one of the bikers writhed on the ground in pain from being shot in the gut, Ray walked up to him, recognizing him from an earlier meet, this one was called Romero who was calling out to Ray.

"Hey man don't leave me like this. Kill me man. I beg you man. I can't stand the pain." Romero was a heavy-weight with these animals and he knew there was no hope for him being gut shot like he was. The pain he felt was a burning sensation which would only be exterminated when he died which could take a few hours. Ray asked him something first.

"You beg do you? Tell me Romero where is my son? Tell nme and I will end it fast for you." Ray was hoping this animal would see he was not fooling around here.

"Sure man." Romero grunted. " he is with Crazy's old lady. See that big chested blonde over there with the rest of the girls, do you see her?"

"I think so." Ray answered.

Ray walked over to where the girls were Ray kicked the other bitches out of the way as he reached out to grab the one that Romero had said had his son. Romero screamed out at Ray in pain,

"I thought you were going to take care of me man?" Ray reminded him,

"I told you what I needed first." Turning around just in time to face Sheryl " The Boobs" Ryder she lunged at Ray with one of Crazy's knives. Grabbing a hold of her arm he twisted it so hard she let the knife fall to the ground while with his other hand he grabbed the front of her shirt ripping it from her body. Pushing hetr to the ground she figured the worse that she would be raped by a cop. It was not his plan with her. Reaching down he hauled the knife out of the ground getting a firm grip on it he asked her,

"Tell me where my son is?" He said it in a way that she could tell he was tired of this chase. Sheryl had a feeling that this was her last day on the earth so instead of coming clean and letting Ray have his son she told him with disdain.

"Go fuck your dead grandmother you fucking rat." Ray looked at her as he punched her straight in the mouth with Sheryl screaming at him,

"What do think you can do to me that has not already been done?" Tearing her top off Ray sat on her chest beating her relentlessly. As Sheryl passed out, he heard Romero whimpering over a little further from him. Ray looked over laughing because he had no wish to see him die easily. " Suffer you bastard." Ray said to himself as he turned his attention back to Sheryl who lay lifeless underneath him. Grabbing her by the hair he hauled out handfuls of hair before throwing her face forward into the tent she would sleep in. Once inside he saw what lay there other than dirty underwear and a change of clothing. But most important in the tent was his son. Ray saw him as Sheryl picked him up then put a knife to the baby's throat.

"Get the fuck out of here or I swear I'll make sure your son does not go with you alive." Sheryl knew this cop would do anything to protect his son but he totally surprised her with what he had to say next.

"Go ahead. I honestly thought he was dead and to tell you the truth I was kind of hoping he did die instead of being raised by the likes of you. So if this is your great plan then do what you have to do, but remember you will follow him shortly."

"I don't believe you cop." Sheryl screamed at him but Ray stood there smiling as he told her more.

"You know all these countless nights I just wanted to hold my son, have him grow up to be whatever he wanted to do in life but you stole that away from me. Now I am a fugitive from the law, every other cop is out there looking for me besides this child has no mother and I have grieved for his soul a thousand times so yes, I can accept his death. His innocence will allow him to go to a better place than where he is right now. So go ahead cut him but I won't be cutting you to kill you, no you don't know what sufferings I have in mind to make you endure."

Sheryl called his bluff sliding the razor sharp blade across the throat of the baby. Blood spurted everywhere in the tent as the lifeless body of Ray's son was discarded like a used piece of clothing. All his rage filled his face as it became distorted staring down at Sheryl as she came to realize in that moment of time her life was about to be forfeited and rightly so for the act of taking the life of an innocent helpless baby.

At once Ray was on top of her beating her unconscious. He continued pulling out clumps of her hair so she would suffer when she was awake from the pain caused by it. Then two more bitches walked into the tent wondering what was going on with Sheryl. Ray moved like a cat grabbing both of then throwing them to the floor he beat them til they passed out. Going back to Sheryl he sat on her sweaty chest thinking of what to do next to make her suffer. Looking around the tent his eyes fell on the knife Sheryl had used to kill his son. Reaching over for it, he stabbed Sheryl in the arms and as the blade when straight to the hilt, he twisted it a half turn before pulling it out then doing the same to the other arm then he followed suit with her legs so she could not move because the pain would be immense. All he had to do now was wake her up so she could feel the pain he inflicted on her. Standing up over her, Ray hauled out his dick and began pissing on her face which brought her back to the land of the living. Tossing her head back and forth to get away from the piss hitting her square in the face, she looked up at Ray who was laughing as he continued to piss in her face. Looking back the other two bitches he had knocked out they lay there oblivious to what was happening to the group of bikers and especially what was taking place with Sheryl their mama who made sure they were well looked after. They depended on her to protect them from the ravages the bikers would inflict on them if they did not please as well as the bikers expected. They were just pieces of meat to the bikers which the girls knew little about as long as they got cock whenever they needed it themselves. Finally he put Sheryl out of her misery by taking the knife and burying it deep into her chest to the hilt, then standing up he looked down at her as her eyes glazed, he raised his leg up stomping down on the knife handle burying it deeper into the dead girl laying before him. Walking around he was looking for something special to tie these bitches up with together because he had a menial job for them. Finding a roll of duct tape he bound one's left arm with the other's right then woke them up by kicking them in the ribs. Moans and groans filled the tent as Ray reached down picking up his lifeless son then turning his attention to the bitches, Ray screamed at them " Get the fuck up now!" Opening their eyes they saw they were taped together oddly so trying to get up was a real chore for both of them as pain shot through their bodies from the kicking in the ribs received from Ray. He was waiting beside them watching them try to get up on their own which was taking too long for him. Reaching down he grabbed one by the hair pulling her to her feet as she cried out in pain as the other one who was bent over on the tent floor in excruciating pain tried to get to her feet but the pain in her ribs was to sore for her to move. Tears ran down their faces as Ray standing beside them laughed at the mess these girls were in.

"Well I see you don't think this is fun anymore since your biker friends left you here alone to deal with me. Where's your laughter now?" Ray screamed at them as he punched the one standing in the gut sending her reeling on her back. Again he reached down grabbing a handful of hair pulling her to her feet.

"I have an important task for you two outside." So pulling the one standing up outside the one having a problem standing had to run on her knees to keep up with them. It was really an awkward situation for both girls as they were lead outside the tent to a serene part of the camp. There under a large oak tree was some fertile soil. Pushing the girls down to their knees he told them.

"I want you to use your hands to dig a hole so I can put my son to rest." The girls did not move so Ray in his anger kicked one of the girls in the mouth shattering her jaw. Blood and teeth came out of her mouth as she knew she had to do as she was told or worse would happen to her. Both were pulling the soil away with bleeding hands as they dug down about three feet deep and three feet wide. Stopping they sat there watching Ray place the infant gently into the hole then looking back at them he motioned for them to bury the child. They obeyed the best they could as Ray sat there knowing he had to get rid of them as well. But he wanted them to feel the hurt and pain he felt in his bones as tears poured down his face. His little son, gone forever was in a much better place hopefully with his wife forever. Bending down Ray tore the jeans off one of the girls with him unfastening his belt he had the idea of sodomizing these girls without any lube, and as soon as he stuck his swollen dick into one he realized she was fucked here before so he pulled out and without pulling up his pants he started beating the girl as her friend looked on suffering from her own abuse. She could do nothing to help her friend who was literally being beatened to death. Then when her movements stopped Ray looked at the other girl then stood up as he fixed his pants he kicked her in the mouth stomping her head until it split in two. Then going back into the tent ray retrieved the knife deeply embedded in Sheryl to bring outside to finish what he had started. Taking the razor sharp knife Ray knelt down cutting the heads off the girls then stuck them on poles he made from fallen trees planting them in the ground then placing a head on each pole. He threw the knife as far as he could into the forest. Falling to his knees Ray began to weep, he felt so tired extremely wiped of strength. After about fifteen minutes of crying he wiped his eyes with the back of his hand and sleeve then pushing himself up he had to return to his car and get the hell out of this killing ground. As he walked back to the car he knew in his mind he would have no peace again until all the bikers were done away with even if he had to chase them to the ends of the earth. But right now he needed to reach his car and sleep as much as he could before being captured by the State Troopers or the Sheriff's department. His business was near completion so he had no desire of being stopped until his work over and done away with. Before leaving he saw what seemed to be another two girls wandering around which made him become justified to what he wanted to do to them. Taking one of them by the hair he dragged her over to the big oak tree where he had just buried his son he tied her to the tree then tearing all her clothes off she had the iq of a three year old so using this to his advantage he made the other one watch as he took little splinters sticking them into the one who was tied up into her boobs.

"What's your name sweetheart?" Ray asked tauntingly. She spat at him which got Ray to back hand her spurting blood out of her mouth. Her twat hung lower showing she was well ridden by the unholy ones who cared less of her health or what she might have felt getting gangbanged as much as possible. She had tattoos burned into her delicate skin which depicted a girl blowing a horse. Some crylic writing was underneath of the picture but Ray did not care, again he asked her, " what's your fucking name?"

"I'm call Sticky Nicky." Was her reply and of course the name fit her. She went on to tell ray what she thought of him.

"These people were my family and you came here to destroy them, have you no mercy?"

"Mercy?? Where was the mercy for my wife, the babysitter or my son? When my wife was repeatedly raped then was smart enough to take her own life, where was the mercy for her?" Ray asked as he continuously punched her. Her friend who was looking on knew it was a matter of time before she would be in the same predictament so she tried to run away from there but Ray was keeping an eye on her as well so as she edged closer to the place where she could finally stand Ray was standing right behind her waiting for her to turn around so he could send her reeling to the ground with a haymaker of a punch which really caused allot of facial damage to the young girl. Dragging her back to the tree by the hair Ray made her watch then decided to get rid of her so helping her stand Ray drove the knife deep into her midsection breaking one of her ribs then giving the knife the little twist he liked doing it was a way for her never to recover from the stab. It tore not only flesh but any veins or arteries close by which would eventually make her die from internal bleeding. She dropped to the ground as her life force seeped out of her body. Ray turned his attention to Sticky Nicky to make sure she was given the same mercy the rest of the victims were given. Gathering dry wood Ray began to pile it all around the girl.

"What are you doing?" She screetched at him but he paid her no attention until he was finished piling it then he had to go back into the tent to find a lighter or some matches he could use to start the fire and roast this one they called Sticky Nicky. When Ray was younger he had met an old Apache indian who related to him the way of using fire to torture someone. Yes it was very painful but efficient in getting the job done properly. Ray knew it worked because he used it while he was in Vietnam.one thing he had to do before lighting the fire was turn her upside down so her hair would burn off her head sending shots of pain throughout her body. So taking the time to undo all the duct tape Ray finally achieved his goal of taping her upside down. Lighting the wood her screams of pain reached a new crescendo so without wasting a moment ray stomped the fire out as she moaned in extreme pain. Then going into the tent ray found a cooler full of beer, taking one he came back out to enjoy his drink as he started the fire once more watching her writhe around in pain screaming obscenities at him as he sat there enjoying the spectacle of this girl burning to death. Suddenly there was a pop which was really the girls brains exploding sending brains out of her ears and mouth. It had been a good day for Ray so far as he watched these little bitches suffer the indignities they so greatly deserved. Looking up there was one more girl left who was walking about stunned at her world falling apart with no bikers around to save her from the disaster she was about to have inflicted on her. Ray came up behind her.

CHAPTER VIII

Speaking out loud so she could hear he startled her as she turned around looking at who was talking to her. As she realized it was the cop she struck out at him scared shitless as she looked those around her, seeing they were all her friends and they lay motionless on the ground for they were all dead. Fear rose throughout her body as she looked at the two girls heads stuck on poles knowing right then and there she was going to be the next victim to the relentless pursuit of a demented cop.

"I'm being good to these whores because there was an agreement I had made that they wouldn't suffer too much." Laughing Ray blocked her blows and let loose his own anger. Punching her so she toppled to the ground he kicked her several times until she lay there looking up at him spewing words which made him laugh even more.

"You won't get away with this. I have friends all over the world. Right now they can hear me cry out for help. You'll see who has the last laugh."

"Shut up dogface. Tell me, who's going to tell them? You from the otherside?" he snickered at what he told her then grabbing her up to himself he told her his aims.

"I am going to fuck you right now." He said laughing as he tore her clothes away. She had a nice body with pert little boobs which he bit causing her to cry out in pain. Throwing her to the ground Ray raped her repeatedly.

"You bastard I hope you burn in hell. I hope your mother gets caught blowing the village priest." Ray let her rage on because he wanted to make this one suffer the most as she was the one who belittled him infront of everyone when he was first beaten by the bikers, when they told him what they did to his wife and how they mistreated the young precious babysitter by cutting her tits off and shoving a piece of wood up her pussy.

"Now bitch you think you are so tough, well let's see just how tough you really are." Taking his time he pulled her hair out in clumps as she tried to fight him but it was no use. He pulled the hair out as blood caked her head and her screams of pain filled his ears. It seemed to give him added strength to watch her try to get away from this animal who had it in his mind to finish her off in some sort of demonic parody which he thought of as he went along. He had gotten rid of the knife so using his own hands to tear the hair out was some great enjoyment as he knew the pain she was suffering under his hands was true. Sitting there watching her pass out from the pain he tied her up then took the time to close his eyes for a long minute, actually he had passed out waking the next morning. The wishes he wanted were fulfilled from the very start of his campaign to rid the world of all these ones who thought just because they had their own law the law of the land did not affect them. So Ray judged them by their own law and carried out executions the same way they did to innocent folk who had a real life with aspirations of making something positive with their lives. These bikers cared little about innocence as they had no room for it. This bitch sitting infront of him was not always this bad, no, it was her involvement with these damn bikers who belittled her each day making her do things a young girl should not have to experience in her life. The disgusting behavior of these bikers as a united throng of illegitimate children not knowing people had a right to be happy and safe took all this away but creating little whores for all their carnal wishes. Too bad Ray thought as he knew he had to finish her off as he did the others. There was no excuse for her to go living. He had to kill her making sure no witnesses of the destructive attitude he carried was found out. Yes when the cops would finally come to take this place apart they would be too late yet they would only find death and destruction already found its mark getting these bikers out of the area but more than that they were to find out someone beat them to the race of killing them off for good. Murder is so easy, Ray thought because he went to war and took life without answering to anyone. When these soldiers come home from doing the terrible things they did to inflict pain and suffering on another human being it stood to be a mainstay in not only their minds but it was now a great part of their being. Some turned to crime, others tried to forget not wanting to talk about it because it was so strong an avenue to live. Yes there were plenty of innocent lives they snuffed out for to fill the void of killing for the day. When Ray was there he had a quota to fill for his commanding officer. Ray was a killing machine that had a quota to fill for his commanding officer so killing gooks was a daily achievement he loved doing but when there were no gooks around he had to fill the void by taking innocent lives making them a martyr which became the very thing why the US lost the war. Ray came home running with his tail between his legs when the gooks started invading Saigon which was an American stronghold. All those young soldiers died for nothing because the United States lost the war. How could you tell a grieving parent it was all for nothing. When Ray got back he faced critisim for being over there in the first place. There were no parades for him when he returned, only riots against him being there in the first place. Shaking his head Ray had to remember why he was in this camp. Why he had to kill this young bitch sitting infront of him. This was all that mattered for now so he had to do so "soon so he could leave without being detected. Before he started with the torture of this girl Ray had to find some food so again he went to the tent. He had found earlier a cooler full of beer but what about some good sustenance to fill his belly? He found some provisions the bikers had left behind like steaks but they were raw so Ray took a couple out built a small fire and placed both of them on a homemade spit which was only big enough for one steak at a time. Fixing it up for himself as it cooked he came back to the girl. She herself hung upside down on a tree so again he built a fire to warm her up which ignited her hair as ray watched her head engulfed in flames he stomped the fire out then hauling out his dick started pissing on her as well. The piss ran down her face which was a welcome relief from the pain the fire had caused. Squatting down to see her face he could tell she was totally delirious from what had happened to her so far. When she came back to the world of the living she sensed Ray was still there so she screamed out at him.

"You rotten fucker. Pay back is a bitch and you will have yours." It was the last thing she ever said as Ray kicked her hard in the throat breaking her windpipe which choked her to death. Going back to the steak he gobbled it down rather quickly which sent a shot of pain through his gut. Not caring he went into the tent bringing out the cooler of beer, opening a beer he drank it down quickly then opened another before searching for and gathering a few weapons to take with him. He left the site going to the car which was well hidden with green leafy branches on top of it. Brushing away the branches he jumped into the vehicle running his hands on the floor around his feet to get the keys. He threw them on the floor just incase he lost them on his excursion. Starting the car up Ray felt better knowing he had disrupted these bikers for now until he met them again.

CHAPTER IX

Word was the bikers had left the States heading for Mexico. Ray needed to get down there himself, finish the job then somehow gather up some cash and leave for Europe. Maybe he would learn how to get by speaking French and take in France for the rest of his life. It was a worthwhile ambition he planned for himself but first things first, he still had the problem of the Unholy Ones to deal with. By all means he would not be able to go anywhere unless he dealt with them first. Looking at himself in the mirror, my god he had aged. These bikers had really did a number on him as he tried to remember when it all began and why. One thing was for certain. He could not take the car. It would stick out like a sore thumb and all the State trooper's would be watching for any hint of it being around. So getting out of the car he opened the trunk to see if there was anything valuable for him to take. Nothing at all unless he wanted to take a tire iron. Shutting the trunk Ray walked away from the car for good. Walking back to where the bikers once were he saw Romero's bike. It was a Harley SuperSport just what he needed to make tracks, easy on gas and easy to maneuver away from the main roads. Starting up the bike Ray looked around for some cash he knew he would need so going through the pockets of those lying dead on the ground he came up with about six hundred dollars which would have to do so off he went again starting up the bike leaving his carnage strewn across the camp. Nothing was alive for him to deal with and anyways the wild animals of the forest would have plenty to eat before the cops came and found this mess. Not caring what took place from now on was Ray's outlook as he lived each day for the day with self- protection. If anything out of the ordinary would arise he would deal with it. But what he needed to do right now was find a way to get into Mexico undetected. So getting out of the state was the first on his agenda as it gave him some freeway to move around without being noticed as the renegade cop the State Troopers were looking for. Now no doubt the FBI would be working the case so his appearance would need some alterations. Going to a small town outside the State he came in looking for a small restaurant which was not too busy so he could get some hot food in his belly. Which inturn would allow him to have a good shit which he did not have for over three days now. All things would come easier now he was out of the firepit and at a loss not of good friends but family. He had a sister in San Diego California who he would never see again. But trying to keep his mind clear so it would be open while on the road he came up with an exquisite plan. Sell the bike then take the bus across the US Mexico border. No one in their right mind would ever think of checking this avenue of escape on him. With the Trooper's car still at the camp most of the Police would think he was still using it so they would be guarding the idea he was traveling only this way. So he kept on trusting his instincts on this afterall he was once a cop, a damn fine cop who was abused by the system. Pulling into a motel off the highway Ray had to get a room. Hopefully he would get one right in the front so he could keep an eye open for any unwanted visitors like the cops or bikers. Going into the main office he was met with an older man who looked like he was surplusing his pension check.

"Good evening sir how may I assist you?" He asked Ray who must have looked like he was in need of a bath.

"Yes I'd like to rent a room for the night if I could." Ray answered. He was tired and needed a good twelve hour sleep to carry him through.

"Why yes. Will it be for just tonight sir or maybe longer?" the old man asked.

"Maybe for two nights. I am bushed riding my bike now for three days and need a bed under me." Ray lied.

"Okay sir. I have room two-twenty open."

"Would that be on the main floor. I saw some empty rooms down there." Ray mentioned as he pointed to the rooms at the end of the hall.

"Would you prefer there sir?"

"Yes so if I feel it's time for me to leave I can leave early in the morning without any problems."

"Very well sir. Do you have any identification?"

"Yes of course." Ray answered as he dug into his back pocket hauling out his wallet. His picture on his driver's licence was good enough.

"Oh I see you are a Police Officer. Good to have you stay here. I should point out there's a rate decrease with our men in blue."

"Well that's good to hear. How much?"

"We usually give Police Officers a twenty-five percent reduction."

"Wow that's quite a saving." Ray told him.

"Yes. We appreciate all the hard work you do. Your bill is sixty-eight dollars for the two nights."

Ray opened his wallet pulling out three twenties, a five and three dollars in change. Giving it to the older man he had to sign his name on the registration card. Doing so he looked for the key ready to almost pass out from exhaustion.

"And here is your key sir. Room sixteen. Have a good night sir." Ray nodded then left the office walking down to the room he just rented. Sticking the key in the door opened easily then pushing the door open a little further, Ray walked into the room closing the door behind himself. Going straight for the bed, he sat on the edge pulling his boots off. His feet gave a strong odor which Ray himself grimaced smelling. A hot shower is what he really needed badly so going to the bathroom he turned the water on getting it hot for him to enjoy. Stripping off in his room he went back to the door to make sure it was locked before he let the water cascade on his sore, tired body. Once naked Ray pulled back the shower curtain stepping into the hot liquid which revitalized his whole being. It sure felt good to wash. There was a small bottle of shampoo he utilized along with a puny bar of soap which came in handy since he had none of his own. For twenty or thirty minutes Ray stayed in the shower letting the heat ease the sore tired muscles of his body. Turning the water off he towel dried then headed for the bed. Turning off the lights he slipped into the soft comfortable bed. Within ten minutes he was sawing logs not waking until the morning came. It was about eleven thirty before he pulled himself out of the bed. He really did not want to get up but he needed the clean clothes he had packed on the bike. So pulling his stinky old jeans back on Ray slipped his shoes back on to go to the bike and fetch his clean clothes. No one was around to give Ray any problems not that he cared, but life had a different road for him as he again stripped down lying on the bed his stomach growled for something to eat. It was great to have a really good sleep but now if he could eat he would be all set. Closing his eyes he slept for another six hours, waking to have a good piss he got up out of the bed, relieved himself then looked at the room he was in. Going to the edge of the bed he pulled on a clean pair of boxer shorts, allowing him to examine his legs which were sore in certain areas and good reason as bruises covered his calves. No ointment to relieve the pain, no pills to cut all the aches he felt. No Ray was a tough breed that would withstand the ailments afflicting his body. It made him stronger in his quest to finish what he had started. Each ache would be justified with the death of one of the bikers he pursued. Pulling on his clean jeans Ray looked around at the pile of clothing he left on the floor. Stuffing the dirty ones back in the bag because even though they were dirty he would need them another day. He pulled out his favorite tee shirt his wife had purchased for him on his birthday. It was totally black with white lettering across the front "CORONER," which read the same across the back on the shoulders. He was the Coroner as far as these bikers were concerned as he did autopsies on living tissue putting it to rest forever. He did not need his jacket on as the heat of the day was sweltering but he would keep it close incase it began to rain. He did not want to get sick while on his quest, no, he wanted to be able to chase down whoever he could, whenever he could. His main purpose right now was to fill the void in his stomach so going to the front office Ray returned the keys then coming back to his room he gathered up his belongings and remembering the gun under his pillow he took this as well, he did not want to be caught without it close at hand so sticking it under his belt in the front he pulled his tee shirt over it then left the room for good. Losing his balance just for a moment, Ray realized he was past the point of starving he needed to fix this problem pronto so going to the bike he started up his bike leaving it idling as he placed his clothes on the back of the seat then climbing on it started to head to the small town just up the highway for some real food. Pulling down the off ramp Ray saw signs of a real good cooked meal waiting for him. Lights filled the evening sky as he followed the trail to this restaurant the signs said was really good food. As he got closer the smell of fresh baked bread filled his nostrils making his mouth salivate as he knew he was getting closer. Up ahead there were a few cars filling the parking lot which did not take Ray long to park the bike. He was beginning to get the shakes so turning off his bike he took two steps at a time to get the hell in there find a table in the front and enjoy whatever he could as his life depended on it. He looked to his left and his right as he stepped into the dimly lit restaurant. The scents of different meals made him wish he were here earlier but he wasn't so he had to make due with the timing of him coming here. Looking again to his left there was a small table with no one taking it so he did. It gave him the access to keep an eye on the bike parked outside in the front which also offered the opportunity to see who would be entering the restaurant. As he gazed outside a pretty young redheaded waitress came to his table.

"May I help you sir?" Ray turned his head slowly to witness a pretty young girl smiling down at him. He had no alternative but to return a smile.

"Yes could I please have a menu?" He needed to order something right away. He went on,

"Could I start with a cup of black coffee?"

"Yes of course." She said as she left his table getting a menu and his coffee she returned placing both infront of him then disappeared again to bring him a set of silverware wrapped in a napkin. Putting a placemat down in front of him Ray was busy trying to sip the hot liquid to ease the pain in his gut.

"Are you ready to order sir or would you like more time?"

"No I am ready now. I'll have the mozerella burger with fries and gravy. Maybe some veggies on the side and a tossed salad with vinaigrette dressing." She wrote this down taking the menu with her as she disappeared into the kitchen. Coming back out she held the coffee pot in one hand as she held a handful of what seemed to be creamers in the other visiting different table to give a refill to the clients eating here. Making her way back over to Ray she asked. " Fill up?"

"Yes please." She filled ray's cup once more with Ray saying, " thank you." Again she went to the kitchen. Within ten minutes Ray had his meal placed infront of him. It all looked so tantalizing so picking up the burger Ray bit into it tasting the savory delight. It felt so good going down so taking another bite he placed the burger back on the plate to try the French fries with gravy he had ordered. A small bottle of ketchup sat infront of him which he shook to get all the liquid inside the bottle mixed together before squirting some on his fries. The gravy was piping hot so he had to be careful not to burn his mouth. Taking the fork out of the napkin it was wrapped in he mixed the gravy all over the fries to allow it to cool down a smidgen before tasting them. As he chewed slowly he noticed outside in the parking lot a cop car checking out his bike, which right now did not fizz him as he took another large bite out of his burger. Aww man it felt good having a meal as he sipped on his coffee he again ate the fries then when he had finished the fries and gravy, when he finished the burger then he tackled the salad which made him feel like a new man. Calling the girl over Ray paid his bill then headed outside to his bike which he started right up then took off for the highway. Now was the time for the business at hand as he made his way through the town streets and lanes to get himself away from this place incase the cops returned looking for the bike when they ran checks on it knowing it belonged to one of the Unholy Ones. They were a bad seed which needed to be separated from the good vibrant seed. Ray did not allow shit like that to hamper his vendetta against the bikers so on he travelled with nothing holding him back to make sure he finished what he had started. One thing Ray wanted to do was go to some bike shop hopefully bikers where he could get rid of the bike for good then take some of the cash to get on a bus heading for Tijuana Mexico and start again on the lookout for the Unholy Ones. Ray wanted all of them. It may take ten twelve years but the wait was really worth it to Ray as he saw an opportunity on the town streets of a motorcycle repair shop. Pulling into the driveway large german shepherd barked relentless at his being there. Out came a biker with a bandana wrapped on his head looking at Ray and his SuperSport bike.

"Can I help you man?" the biker asked as Ray turned off his bike getting off and walking towards him.

"Yeah. I'd like to see if I can sell my bike?"

"Why? What's wrong with it?"

"Oh there's nothing wrong with it but I am getting older and looking at picking up a small car." Ray lied.

Coming over to look at the bike. The biker kneeled to have a good look at the pistons running his hands across the bike he looked up at Ray asking, " how much?"

Watching him intently Ray told him, " make me an offer?"

"Well, the best I can do is take it for a spin to see if there's anything it may need. Is that alright?"

"Sure go ahead. Does your dog bite?"

"No just a barker unless you attack me." He said as he laughed a little.

"No worries there." Ray said as he watched the biker start up the bike taking off on one of the lonely streets. Ray waited patiently for about fifteen minutes until he heard the roar of the bike coming back to him. The biker was well pleased with the way the bike held itself.

"Well what do you think?" Ray asked as he wanted to get the hell out of this place into the warmth of Mexico, set up himself in a hacienda and make plans to exterminate the Unholy Ones.

"Well this bike is well worth twenty-five thousand but I don't have that kind of cash so I suggest you take it elsewhere and get your money's worth." These were not the words Ray was expecting so he made up a line the biker would no doubt jump at.

"I'll tell you what, say you give me ten grand cash and take it off my hands. You yourself said it's worth more than that and this way you get a deal."

"Ten grand?? That's all? Sure I'll give you ten grand for it. Come on inside and let's do the paperwork."

Ray followed him into the office as he looked around seeing parts for bikes and bikes being created or worked on which were half done. The dog came up to Ray sniffing him then returned to the box in the corner where there was a small mat to lie on.

"So do you have any ID?" The biker asked as he had some sort of book open. Ray hauled out Romero's wallet showing the biker the driver's licence. Picking it up he examined the pic as the pic showed a younger man than what Ray looked like.

"Is this your pic man?"

"Yeah. It was taken a few years ago when youth was a better place for me."

"Well I know what you are saying. I'll be forty this summer. Can't believe the time has slipped away so fast."

Ray said nothing only interested in getting his hands on some ready cash. Then the biker surprised him.

"I only have ninety-eight hundred in cash so I will write you a check for a couple of hundred. Sorry about that but that's the best I can do." Ray did not mind as he watched the biker count out the ninety-eight thousand.

"You need me to sign anything?" Ray asked knowing full well he had to sign the transaction form to have the bike transferred to the biker.

"Yeah if you could, right here." The biker pointed to the line for Ray to sign. He only knew the dead unholy One as Romero so he signed Romero legibly but the last name was a scribble. It was done. Ray left the bike shop with nearly ten thousand bucks in his pocket then had to go to the main street of the town to find out where he would catch a bus to Mexico. Going out to the bike he retrieved his clothing and turned to shake hands with the biker who just got one incredible deal on the bike or so he thought as the cops were looking for the bike and it's driver. Ray continued walking until he heard some music coming his way from a local night spot where plenty of cars were parked. Funny he did not notice this place on the way in to the garage where he sold the bike. There were a few people milling about outside which looked like they were smoking cigarettes or pot because they kept passing a lit small rolled cigarette around to each other. Why not? Ray thought to himself as he meandered over to the bar to have a drink. It had been several years since he ever tied one on and with a pocket full of cash he might even get lucky enough to meet some bitch and get laid. Going to the front door, he nodded at the ones outside enjoying what they were smoking and yes it was pot as the pungent smell told him. Ray remembered back in college the pot he used to smoke and preferred to see kids smoke that instead of crack or crystal meth. Smoking pot was harmless and needed more encouragement from the government. As a matter of fact the way Ray looked at it, if pot were legal to smoke it would get rid of the national debt in five years. Pushing the door open he stepped inside. Most of the people here were young enough to be his children so looking around for a good spot to sit he saw one but it was way in the back away from the bar. Squeezing in through a crowd of kids Ray finally got to the bar.

"What'll it be sir?" the young bar tender asked him.

"I'll have a Jack Daniels double straight and a bud." This was always Ray's favorite drink. A Jack Daniels whiskey with a beer to chase it down. Hauling out of the pocket which had the least cash Ray slapped down a twenty with four fifty as change. Pushing it to the barkeep Ray made his way to the table in the back. There were a few eyes on him as he sat down but mostly others went about their business without even noticing him. Soon as Ray sipped on the beer, a young blonde girl came over to talk with him.

"May I?" She asked motioning if she could join him at the table.

"Sure." Ray answered as he took his bag off the seat for her to sit down.

"I haven't seen you here before. From out of town?"

"Yeah I had a little business to do but I will be leaving in the morning."

"Got a place for the night?" She asked smiling but looking him straight in the eyes.

"No not yet. I saw a motel on the highway so I may have to call a cab."

"No need for that. I'm having a few people over why not join us. If you pass out or want to crash there you are more than welcome." This was the best offer Ray knew he was going to get so he took her up on it.

"Okay it sounds like fun. Can I buy you a drink?"

"Sure. I'll call the girl over or if you let me have a twenty I'll get you another beer and I'll pick up a vodka." Ray reached into his pocket hauling out three twenties so giving her one she disappeared into the crowd but within minutes came back carrying the drinks. She smiled as she got closer to him then sat down at the table as they chatted about small things to get to know each other better.

"By the way my name is Ray." He said as they never really introduced themselves.

As she held he hand out to shake his she told him, " I'm Peggy. Glad to meet you Ray." After they were finished their drinks she stood up motioning him to join her so when he did she grabbed his hand to start walking through the crowd to leave. Once outside she turned to face him kissing him full on the mouth.

"C'mon Ray let's get the hell out of here and have our own party. She was walking over to a Jaguar but as Ray saw it she was in no way good to be driving.

"Maybe you should let me drive." He mentioned so turning towards him she tossed him the keys telling him, "Go ahead." They climbed into the car as she directed him to the place where she lived he parked in the driveway and started to get out of the car but she pulled him back giggling.

"Let's not go in right yet." Ray returned to his seat closing the door as Peggy reached over rubbing his dick she pulled down the zipper having his cock pop out she licked it then slipped it into her mouth. Ray loved the way she licked it even when she sucked it. It took about ten minutes when Ray exploded in her mouth and she swallowed all of it, even licking it clean. Looking up at him she told him.

"Some girl friends of mine are here so I just wanted to see if you were the type of man who could take care of us."

"How many are there?" Ray asked not knowing if he could get gangbanged and supply all the girls what they wanted.

"Four or actually five counting you. You think you can be up for it?" Peggy teased as she opened her side of the car getting out. Ray followed suit watching she did not fall or hurt herself but man she gave good head. Going inside there were three girls playing with each other as their gaze fell upon him they came to him helping him take off his clothes. They were really pleased to see him naked as he stood there with his dick starting to bob from the soft touches these girls were giving him. Soon his dick was rigid as one of the girls slipped it into her mouth the others watched him close his eyes in ectasy and begin to swing his hips back and forth. She took it out before he exploded to make sure the other girls had a try with him each of them gave him head until he exploded in a warm, wet mouth. It was like playing Russian roulette with his dick being the gun. Soon they had him on his back riding him with each girl taking a turn it wasn't long before Ray was tiring out. So when the party was over a couple of hours later Peggy lay on top of him telling him softly.

"I want you to take a warm bath with me upstairs and then you can towel dry me." Ray smiled at her as his thoughts of lust made his dick start to bob once again. Peggy noticed this and instantly got up on top of him riding him until he came four more times filling her pussy with his precious juice. He could not fuck anymore so he got up with her heading upstairs as he carried his clothes, he was not about to leave his money for someone else to come in and rob him.

Peggy ran a tub of warm water then pushed Ray on the bed. It was a four poster bed which gave plenty of room for romping around.

"Tell me what you are thinking?" Peggy asked as she lay beside him.

"I am wondering why I was the lucky one to be picked by you. I mean there were quite a few good looking young guys there, why me?"

"Well because you are older, more mature. You know how to handle a woman when she really needs a swollen cock in her. Those young guys can fuck but leave us ladies hanging for more. They have their orgasm not achieving one for us, just hauling it out then disappearing. It's not fair so I figured an older guy would not do that and you didn't you were rather sweet to us all." Getting up she called out to him,

"C'mon Ray let's take a warm bath." Ray came into the bathroom finding Peggy had already gotten in the bath so stepping in the warmth of the bath felt good against his bare skin. She had a wash cloth to wash herself completely then took it to wash him completely. Just laying there holding each other Peggy fell asleep so Ray knowing they would catch a cold pulled the plug on the bath then stood up to get out, she opened her eyes seeing what was happening so she too got out of the tub to let Ray towel her down. Going into the bedroom relaxed they held each other close through the night.

Ray decided to take it easy for a few days before making any rash decisions about what he had to do. This way the heat from the cops would quiet down so he could move freely to anywhere he wanted to go. When the cops realized the bikers had left America they left the States disrupted forever so the Police along with the FBI had a statute passed through the Senate that bikers were not allowed to go to small towns ever again. This of course was being viewed by other larger motorcycle groups as an intolerance caused by the Unholy Ones. So they themselves would take the Unholy Ones apart waging a war against them if they ever came to the States again. Ray on the otherhand, had his eyes set on going to Mexico to finish off any member of the Unholy Ones himself but right now he was enjoying the virtues of Peggy. He needed to hold a woman close to himself at night like he did each night with his wife, his wife, whenever he thought of her it made him shed tears but when he was alone never would he let Peggy get so deep into his heart for Claire was his one and only true love. No one else could ever fill the void he felt when not with Claire or his son who was snuffed out by Sheryl. Yes Ray had a hand in it but he could not look after the boy now he was on the run. It was better to put the child to rest which meant he was at peace with the world. The world which was changing each day for the worse so what kind of upbringing could Ray expect to give his son? No he let the days pass then it became weeks. Peggy had grown quite fond of having Ray around giving her the needed sex she had planned for herself each week. Yeah she did not mind sharing him with her friends and he didn't seem to mind balling the girls as long as it was at Peggy's residence. Any sex outside the home was strictly done with Peggy because she was giving Ray a chance to get his thoughts together for the big move he had to do to complete his task. How he would break off he did not know, maybe just leave without a word so he would not have to get into the meat of the problem he faced. Ray's hatred for the bikers was something he used to carry on in life. Sometimes there were anger bursts but only when he was alone. He could not allow himself to divulge the true feelings he had for the future. It had been nearly two years since Ray and Peggy teamed up so the relaxed time he had helped him get over the bruising and sore spots across his body he had from his run in with the bikers at their camp. It was as if it were yesterday when all of this happened. He clearly remembered cutting the heads off the two little bitches sticking their heads on poles. It really wasn't their fault. They had been abused by the Unholy Ones belittled each day to become the misfits the bikers desired for carnal pleasures then they had to work the streets bringing home all the cash they made along with the porno movies they were forced to make to increase the capital the bikers needed for the drugs they did. It was a terrible way to live life but these girls lost all respect they had for themselves or for anyone they came in contact with. Ray began to feel a little guilty for treating them this way but at the moment he was not in his right mind either. Lying on the bed waiting for Peggy to get home from work he thought about leaving more and more.

It was raining outside which did not help matters as Ray was feeling depressed on what he had to be doing in the next few days. What really made matters worse was the fact that Peggy knew about what he did even mentioning it to him.

"You know love, I have been wondering why you did not tell me about those bikers you killed." It totally caught Ray with his pants down. How the hell would she know what he was involved with. He thought it was a well-kept secret.

"What the hell are you talking about?" Ray answered trying to be naïve to her questioning.

"C'mon Ray. I heard what had happened a few years ago just about the time you waltzed into the club. An older cop who went bad on a killing spree, it's just too much a coincidence you just happened to be there. Not like I'm going to squeal on you but it does raise some important questions if we are going to be an item."

Ray had no choice but to seal this mess now then get the hell out of there for good. He had about seven thousand dollars left which he would need to make his disappearance happen.

"Who else did you talk to about this?" Ray asked because if others knew then his safety was in jeopardy.

"No one honey. I don't believe it's anyone else's business. But I want all the juicy details." She said as she crawled into his lap. Ray finalized in his mind to be rid of her before night ended. He had to leave by his own accord which meant he could not take her car but make his way by himself. They would put a trace on the car realizing he was trying to get across the border then his safety would be done away with as the Mexican authorities would transfer him back to the States where he would get the death penalty for what he had done. No this had to be the night to finish her sand move on and with luck he would be in Mexico tomorrow. Standing up Peggy fell to the floor. He turned away from her whimpering as she had banged her left knee on the floor displaying an instant bruise. He cared little of her well-being right now only thinking about what he must do.

"Baby that hurt." She cried out to him but he was busy in the bedroom packing his clothes. As she hobbled to the bedroom she saw him packing.

"Baby what's going on? Are you leaving me?"

"I can't stay here. Your big mouth will no doubt blurt out what you know which will be very detrimental to my freedom. It's just too bad you had to spill what we had together. Your interference has destroyed any feelings I have for you."

"You can't be serious. Then it was you who killed those kids. I'm calling the Police." She said as she turned going for her cell phone. Ray was right there to grab it out of her hand slapping her so she fell to the floor.

"I never wanted to harm you but you leave me no other choice. My job with those fucking bikers is not over yet and I will not allow you to ruin what I have planned for years. Too bad because I believe I fell in love with you. If it means me killing you to be free then so be it!" Ray stepped towards her grabbing her in a headlock then twisting her neck to hear a giant crack she fell to the floor lifeless. Going to her purse he grabbed what cash she had then getting his things he turned the lights down low, locking the door before leaving for good. Walking down the deserted street he saw the bus stop he needed to reach and hopefully did not have to wait long for the bus to take him south of the border. Waiting for nearly two hours was a terrible time for Ray as he wanted to get on the bus without meeting any of Peggy's friends in the process. Trouble was one could not predict when the stupid bus would show up so he made himself a make-shift seat and plopped down. If he were to wait he may as well be comfortable. Closing his eyes he thought of the wonderful times he had with Peggy until she opened her big mouth about his past. Loose lips sink ships and he was not about to have his ship sunk because some stupid broad had an agenda to reopen the past. Looking down the road to his left he saw a vehicle coming up his way maybe about two miles down the road heading his way so getting himself up he saw it was the bus. Gathering his belongings he waved the bus down which stopped just in front of him opening the door which took Ray tree seconds to board. It looked loaded down so looking at the driver he dealt with him.

"This bus go to Tijauna?"

"Yes it does sir. Do you have a passport or identification as we need to go through customs." He was a well groomed man who looked pretty sharp in his uniform. His steel grey eyes beamed at Ray as he added a smile of whiter than white teeth.

"I'm prepared." Ray told him softly. He could have been gruff but what good would that do but draw attention to himself.

"How much?" Ray asked.

"To Tijauna it is forty dollars sir." Ray dug into his right hand pocket hauling out three twenties, two tens and a five. Going through the bills Ray handed the driver two twenties shoving the other cash back into his pocket. Finding a seat in the front was hardly a chore as most everyone wanted to sit in the back. Sharing the double seat was an old lady who looked like she had better days. Wrinkles covered her face and Ray could see she was a grumpy old bat who liked dictating orders to those around her. He thought of her being his grand- mother who would cringe if she only knew. Sitting on the aisle seat as she was sitting close to the window, Ray plopped down holding his bag in his lap. In the bag was the rest of the cash he would need to make a life in Mexico so he wasn't about to let it get out of his grip. The rip took longer than Ray thought it would be because there were plenty of stops on the way down south. Finally before getting to the border there was an opportunity for everyone to stretch their legs and use the washroom if needed. Ray was no exception as he held the piss he desparately needed for sometime now. Taking the lead of getting off the bus he headed straight to the washroom locking the door behind himself he relieved himself then washed up. Paper towels were what hung there to dry his hands and face as he splashed water on his face looking into the mirror to see how time had ravaged his skin. He was getting older from all the stress he had to go through along with the beatings he took it really did a number on him. Drying off he reached for the lock to open it then walk out of the washroom for the next guy. Going outside the station Ray stuck his hand in his left front jacket pocket to haul out the remaining cigarette he had saved for an occasion like this. Lighting it up he walked away from the crowd of people with the same idea of lighting up. He did not want to talk to anyone as he waited patiently to get back on the bus and complete his traveling. Once everyone got back on the bus Ray waited until he was the last one to board before the driver. Getting comfortable in his seat Ray waited until the driver started up the bus, then closing the door continued down the highway towards the border. Closing his eyes ray seemed comfortable sitting there waiting for the extreme exit from the States as he started to doze off. Soon he was being nudged in the side from the old lady sitting beside him waking him so he turned to her to look to see if they were at the border and this was her way of waking him up. Still driving down the road Ray was having a good sleep and this old bag woke him.

"Why did you hit me in the ribs?" Ray asked as he looked at her.

"You were snoring. I hate listening to people snore." She told him honestly. Ray closed his eyes again but not for sleep, just to keep from talking to her again. Too bad, he thought, she was saved from having other people on the bus because he would probably give her a shot in the head for her actions of waking him up. Leaning forward, Ray rubbed the sleep out of his eyes then yawned. As he stretched he nearly hit her in the head which he realized was something he did not care about. Getting his position back in the seat Ray adjusted his sitting to get as comfortable as he could as he gazed out the window to see nothing but barren land out there. Every once in a while a patrol car could be seen telling Ray he was getting close to the border. Then as they came around the next crest lights up ahead told everyone on the bus they were approaching the US-Mexico border. Sitting up in his seat he saw it was going to take some time before they crossed as plenty of cars ahead of them were being checked as they went into and left Mexico. He remembered his days as a cop but this border job was one he would never do. The same thing each day of checking cars was not his cup of tea. No he enjoyed the chase of criminals throughout the counties and apprehending dangerous criminals who figured crime did pay. His arrests were a matter the town appreciated as his busts were true busts, there was no one getting off on technitalities which some crooks did. Ray's arrests were solid arrests he took pride in upholding the law until the law screwed him letting the bikers eliminate his family. Never again would he become a cop eventhough he kept his badge for purposes beyond his control. The badge would help him get out of sticky situations but in his heart it was all a façade. As the bus creaped closer to the border the driver came to a complete stop off to the side so the bus driver turned off the ignition then opened the door so passengers could depart off the bus to get checked at the border. Standing Ray made his way off the bus to be counted as sheep to enter Mexico without a hitch. As he stood outside the bus an officer came up to him telling him to enter the building to the right where all the passengers were guided to fill out a form telling the border police why they were going to Mexico. Each one was searched as part of the program to find out if any of the passengers was carrying contraband. Once inside the building there were different rooms where passengers were lead to be skin searched. Ray realized he had a gun on himself and should have discarded it while on the bus but now it was too late to rid himself of it plus he had a large amount of cash in his jacket pocket. Was this going to be as far as he got? Going into one of the rooms he was asked to empty his pockets. Ray was fucked. If the gun came into question he could be charged not only with possession of a firearm but illegally trying to bring it in to a foreign country. What the hell was he going to do? Ray did not have a prayer as his wanted poster hung on the wall yet it was a picture of him in full uniform as a Police Officer. Yes he was a lot younger in the picture but he wasn't dealing with fools. These were seasoned officers guarding the border, seasoned enough to pull their guns out as soon as Ray was in a room. There were four officers who shouted at him.

"Get on your knees. Hands on the top of your head." Ray had no recourse but to listen to what they were telling him as their guns were cocked and aimed to the back of his head. Kneeling down Ray placed his hands on top of his head like they had instructed him. One of the guards who had stripes telling everyone he himself was a sergeant leaned forward at Ray telling him.

"You aren't too bright coming into my district. Did you think you could just ride into Mexico without an alarm sounding off. Ray Blue you are wanted for multiple murders and dishonoring Police nationwide." Placing cuffs on Ray they lead him to a small building where there were holding cells. He wasn't alone. There were four others in cells waiting for someone from the FBI to come take them away. Placing Ray in one of the cells he was pushed in then he had to stick his hands through the small opening in the bars to get the cuffs taken off. Was this the end of the road for him as he knew too well if he went to trial he would be sentenced to death. No, Ray's mind was working over time as he though of different ways to get out of here. The other inmates just gazed upon him wondering why he was in this place with them.

"Hey amigo. What were you carrying?" A young Mexican asked as everyone laughed. Ray failed to see the humor then openly told them his story.

"I wasn't carrying anything. I am wanted for murder in Philo county in Arizona for killing a few cops. I see you want to join them." Ray said as he smiled at the young Mexican. Then he went on.

"When I get out of here because of your laughter I will kill each of you fucking spics." They straightened up in their cells looking at Ray telling him.

"You better get out because if I am free and see you again I will show you how we treat pieces of shit like you in Mexico. I corumba, the pain you will experience will go off the charts. Do you happen to know who I am?"

Ray shook his head slowly, no. as the Mex went on.

"Y ou are speaking with Ramone Hernadez. I am known throughout Mexico as the greatest bandit of all time."

"Is that so?" Ray asked, " then tell me you stupid fucker if you are so great, then why you are locked up in a cell?"

"You still do not realize you cannot talk to me like I am some peasant off the streets of Puerto Vallarta, no my friend I will show you real Mexican justice. So you best leave when you can because they will come for us and stick us in the jail where my brothers wait for me then we will see who you call spic to." The door to the room opened to show the faces of three border patrol guards bringing in trays of food for the prisoners. Feeding the Mexicans first they waited to serve Ray last opening his tray to show baked beans when one of the officers spit a luggie on Ray's meal.

"That's what we think of dirty cops." Laughing they left the building so the inmates could enjoy their meal.

"So you are a dirty cop?" The Mexican started. Ray was not hungry but he was glad he had a fork spoon in his possession. Not caring about the ramblings of the Mexicans Ray took the spoon fork to the wall pressing with all his strength the handle against the wall sharpening the handle for it to become a lethal weapon. When the officers came back to collect the trays Ray threw his meal on one of the officers which got him really pissed. Taking the keys he opened Ray's cell while the other two had their guns out but not cocked. A terrible mistake which would cost the officers their lives. As the officer willing to pay Ray back for the meal being tossed on him came into the cell Ray jumped to his feet holding the sharpened spoon fork handle to his throat.

"Okay you two if you don't want your friend here to be pushing up daisies then drop your guns because I have nothing to lose if I kill another one of you fuckers." They dropped their guns then backed up as Ray pushed the officer he held hostage towards them. Picking up one of the guns they asked him a simple question.

"How far do you expect to get?" This place is flooded with officers and they will shoot you dead."

"Maybe," Ray began, " but I will take you fuckers with me." Pointing the gun at them he told them the same they told him.

"Get on your fucking knees and put your hands on your head." They complied because theis guy who held the gun was a killer who shot several officers so why would they make a wrong move to get killed? No each of them were married with children and they knew one wrong move would make gtheir wives widows. Collecting their holsters where extra clips for the guns were housed he motioned them into the cell themselves which they did as he asked. Then taking one out who was older, Ray told him matter of factly.

"I want you to strip down." The officer began to unbutton his shirt looking around to see if there was some way of stopping this mad man. Off came his shirt then his vest which Ray grabbed a hold of. Then came the pants which Ray threw into a corner. Motioning for the officer to get back into the cell he did the same way to the other officers until Ray held three vests. Trying them on he found one that fit perfectly then pulling his tee shirt back on he covered the vest, then speaking to the officers again he told them.

"I am going to take your ID and wallets because you took my cash. I will need it to get where I am going in Mexico." The other four inmates wanted to be free as well so they began talking to Ray in a soft voice.

"Hey amigo. Don't forget us we can help you. Why not take us with you?" Ray stood there for a moment thinking about what they said but he did not need them unless he thought he use them for a diversion to get him free from the border. Walking to their cell he cocked back the hammer on the gun pointing it at them which they thought he was going to kill them until he unlocked the cell to release them from their jail. One of the Mexicans picked up the sharp spoon fork lying on the floor as a weapon which made Ray back up enough to watch what he was about to do. Opening the cell of the officers the Mexican jabbed at one of the officers stabbing him in the neck with blood spurting on the other two officers who cringed in fear. Then stabbing the officers several times the officers fell to the floor dead which was not in Ray's plans for his escape but dead men tell no tales. Slamming the cell door shut, he locked thee killer mex in with the guards he just killed.

"Hey what are you doing?" they screamed at Ray who made his way out of the small building into the desert before him. Figuring the border police would kill those spic for what they did to their fellow officers it was just one less thing for Ray to deal with. He had two guns leaving one on the floor so if the spics could somehow free themselves they would have a weapon to try to regain their freedom. If not they would be caught in the cell with three dead officers and their prints all over the weapon they used. Ray was only interested in saving his own bacon not looking out for other inmates to be with him he did not trust.

CHAPTER X

Opening the door to the small building slowly, Ray peeped outside watching the border guards checking cars. He stepped out rather quickly making sure there was no influence of causing a scene as he took the first right which lead to the back of the buildings. Putting his jacket on he had taken from one of the guards in the cell Ray wanted carry as little as possible as he had one of the handguns in his right hand which would come in handy if he needed to use it. There was no question at all if he would use it. If it meant killing a border cop for him to gain his freedom then the border cop would die. Out back here, it lead him to the kennels where the dogs were constantly barking which he used as a screen to flee the premises. Their barking covered him as he ran by the kennels to the place where the guards parked their cars. It was good fortune for him right now because here was an opportunity for him not only to steal a car but get the hell out of the area deep into Mexico. He would have to change his American dollars to pesos then get a place in no man's land to live his life freely. Ray knew very little Spanish but he could get by discussing rent, where to buy food and maybe pick up a senorita for a night's frolicking. Right now though he had to open the car door which was not hard because the border police never locked their car doors. Why would they? Ho would steal a cop's car? Ray slid into the car reaching for the gear shift to put it in neutral as he got back out pushing the car from his knees to have it move to the open road where he would again push it out of sight to hot wire the car then take off to a better place. Once on the road there were plenty of immigrants heading for the border with hopes of starting a new life in America. Ray had to be careful as he passed them as some walked on the road not caring there was a car coming at them. Just what he needed now was to hit and kill one of these peasants to draw the whole Police force upon him. No Ray used special care slowing down to a trickle of speed until he had passed them all then sped up to move as far away as possible. Driving for what seemed an eternity the sky was turning to orange which told him the evening hours were about to be upon him so he kept on always checking to see how he was doing for gas. Right now he was down to a quarter of a tank which meant he would have to stop soon and refill. Up ahead on the flatlands was a small gas station with several people sitting under the trees for shade having siestas. Ray pulled in hoping he could get the car filled then mosey on along trying to find a place to hold up for a few weeks before moving onwards. Pulling up tpo the pumps no one came out to service him so he helped himself. Getting out he went to the back of the car to open the gas tank cover then taking the hose stuck it in to the car and started pumping gas into the vehicle. Out came an older man with a sombrero tied around his neck.

"May I help you senor?" He asked as he walked up to Ray.

"Yeah I'm just filling the tank. My first time to Mexico so tell me is there any small towns around here looking for someone to rent a room?"

"We have a room here senor. You can have two hot meals a day and shower for two hundred pesos a month." Ray thought about it as the gas pumped into the car. Walking to the other side of the car was a squeegee which he used to clean the dust off the windows. Then coming back to the old man he asked him straight.

"Any place for me to lose this car?"

The old man smiled showing he had very few teeth left in his mouth then he answered Ray.

"I can arrange for the car to go missing if you like senor for only five hundred pesos."

Five hundred pesos Ray thought would be like fifty dollars american, not bad for his independence and right now he had the cash to pay him so nodding in agreement he followed the old man into the gas station which turned out to be the house of he and his family of eight. His wife was a large woman who had these kids which were three boys and five girls. The youngest was a boy he was four years old but the girls were from the age of fifteen to twenty-three. Ray looked them over seeing they were not the cutest but he would bang them if need be. Spewing off in Mexican the old man told his wife and family that Ray would be staying with them for a little while. Ray needed to have a shit so he went to the old Mexican asking, " where's there bathroom?" The old Mexican took him to an outhouse in the back which Ray entered but the stench of rotted shit filled his nostrils which was not an appetizing scent. Ray really needed to use the bathroom so in he went pulling down his jeans he sat on the warm seat letting nature take its course. It felt good to be able to relax from the storm winds he had been in earlier in the day. He thought about the one called Ramone Hernandez and how he was faring being locked up in the cell with his compadres along with the dead border control officers. Were they dead? Ray did not know nor did he care. All that was on his mind was getting something good to eat and having a relaxing sleep and the hell with everyone who did not like it when he snored. It was late afternoon when the old man came forward to tell Ray dinner was being served. Tamales, tacos and a good shot of tequila to wash the food down. These people had very little but they were content with everyday life until the bikers showed up.

"YAH ARIBA!" Came a shot out front along with the roar of bikes which meant bikers were here to harass the poor man and his family. There were six of them filling their bikes and figuring they did not have to pay so Ray sat back waiting for these assholes to enter the home and try to hurt the girls. It did not take long before one of the girls sat by a window showing her tits to them which made them make up their minds they were coming in to sample the wares of these young girls. Ray had his gun in his hand just incase these hard cases thought they could rule over everyone. The girl who showed her tits was the oldest, she was twenty-three, a virgin who wanted to get laid before she died. These bikers were game for some free sex eventhough she was ugly they cared little because to them it wasn't the face you fucked it was the fuck you faced. The old man tried to stop them but was beaten by them as they moved into the house breaking jars, smashing things up so Ray stood to intervene. He could not believe his eyes it was Coaster causing all this grief so going out the back Ray sneaked to the front. Taking aim he shot both bikers outside guarding the bikes which got the other bikers outside wondering who was firing a gun. Ray stood in the shadows watching them as they went to their fallen buddies looking around for the guilty party who would have the audacity to do such a thing to a member of the Unholy Ones. Finally Coaster's eyes fell upon Ray which was a total shock to him so getting on his bike to get the hell out of there Ray shot him in the back of the head. His three friends stood where they were not moving so Ray would not think they were retaliating. But it was no use as Ray lowered the gun to their belly line shooting the three of them in the gut. The old man came stumbling out yelling at Ray.

"What are you doing? Do you not know many will come here looking at us as the enemy? I must ask you to leave now, save yourself." Ray looked at him and the family as they were shocked Ray had killed the bikers. Now they were scared but Ray smiled at them telling the old man.

"Let them come. I will be ready for them. You go in with your family but send out your oldest girl." The old man complied with what Ray had told him sending out Maria the eldest. She looked at Ray not knowing English only Mexican. Calling out the old man Ray told him,

"I want to say something for your daughter to understand." He nodded at Ray and began to translate to his daughter what Ray wanted to say.

"It was very foolish of you to show your tits to the bikers. Do you see what they did to your parents home? If you want a man then you can sleep with me tonight, I will treat you alright. And when the bikers come here again please do not do this action again. It will cause a lot of trouble to you and your family."

She smiled at Ray as she knew she was getting laid tonight. She had seen pictures of men with women even saw her father and mother together wishing she could have a man grunt over her. Well her prayers had been answered as she looked at Ray's crotch noticing a bulge which she wanted to feel inside herself. Walking over to ray she took him by the hand to lead him to her bedside where she rubbed the bulge with her left hand as she pulled him down on top of her. As they were getting it on the rest of the family took the dead bikers outside town and buried them in the sand. Taking their bikes to the back where they had a large garage they put the bikes there hoping the other bikers did not notice them there.

It was a long day as Ray and the old man sat waiting for the worse to happen but nothing did take place except the eldest daughter who lost her virginity to Ray was serving him with whatever he needed for food and cleaning of his clothes. It was as if he were married to the girl which was something Ray did not want right now. He needed no ties until his session with all the bikers was completed. He had come to Mexico for a reason even killing border police who were on the hunt for him which they thought would be easy for a recapture since he stole an officer's car. An All Points Bulletin ran throughout Mexico and for the general public there was a hefty reward of one hundred thousand American dollars for his arrest and conviction. The border police knew if he were recaptured he would never reach trial as they had their own justice league to take care of matters burying him in the sands of the plentiful desert of Mexico. Ray on the other hand had no doubt he would not be able to leave Mexico after all this was done but he had thoughts of South America to live the rest of his days. He sat on a chair in the shade thinking of all that had transpired since losing his wife, son and babysitter. At least in his heart they were at peace never having to deal with the pressures of life ever again. Maybe there was a heaven for righteous people so they would gain entrance there but his righteousness was lost when he decided to be the executioner of these terrible animals that caused ruin to everyone's life. They seemed to poison everything that had a good purpose so they could have their fun. Well their fun was about to end shortly as Ray checked what he needed to maintain his freedom. Looking out to the right, Ray saw a large dust cloud coming their way which startled ray as he got up going into the house to get his weapons. It caught everyone off guard as now they expected the worse to be taking place. As the vehicles got closer to the little station it was apparently two Mexican checking out every possible hiding place for the fugitive Ray Blue. The reward had a lot to do with it as these Mexican police pulled into the small driveway of the gas bar. The Lieutenant jumped out of the first vehicle barking orders to his men to search the premises. Five officers carrying machine guns ran into the house yelling at the old man and his family then finally having them brought outside and lined up in a single file the Lieutenant questioned them about the whereabouts of Ray Blue. He apparently did not like the answer he got from the old man so came up to him punching him in the belly making the old man drop to his knees. The rest of the family tried to console the old man as the guards shot several rounds into the air to regain their attention and have them stand quietly as the Lieutenant questioned further. Sending two of his men to the house to search it, Ray used his skills to wait just outside the back door to get the officers out there by rattling some piece of wood dangling g on a pole. Coming out they crouched down silently to see what would cause the wood to make such a noise then when they appeared outside behind the house, Ray used a sharp long knife which was just a littlen shorter than a sabre to slash the throat of one of the officers. As the other turned to see his partner he was not there but Ray was. Driving the knife deep into the officer several times this officer joined his partner. " Now the odds are better." Ray said to himself as he made his way to the front of the house to witness two more officers wrestling two of the young daughters to the ground. Stepping out, Ray fired two shots killing the Lieutenant and a fellow officer as the two on the ground with the daughters were caught with their pants down. Their weapons were in the car which they looked for as Ray stood above them, ready to kill them for what they were doing.

"Filthy pieces of shit. Get the fuck up now!" Ray screamed at them. They lay their motionless as they did not understand Ray until the old man came and told them what Ray had said. Both began to blurt out they were just following orders. But they caught the drift when Ray cocked the gun aiming it at them so they pushed themselves up to a standing position with their pants down to their ankles Ray looked at the old man saying,

"You mete out the justice." Tossing the knife on the ground before the old man everyone could see the blood on it from the other two Ray had killed. As ray looked at his prisoners he had no recourse except to do away with them as well. Going to the old man he told him his problem and the only way out of this mess these Mexican police had caused. On the second jeep the police were riding, there was a fifty calibre sub-machine gun so Ray came up with a brilliant solution to the problem at hand.

"We need to load the bodies into the jeeps, take them somewhere far away from here so nothing will come back on you and let them sit in the jeep as if they are taking a break. Then we must allow the bikers to think they can kill these hapless soldiers taking their machine gun jeep as a reward for what they did. Of course they will be stupid enough to ride the jeep around because with a fifty calibre machine gun in their possession who would bother them. When the police stumble on the dead bodies of their fellow officers and word gets out the bikers have such a killing weapon, what do you think will happen?"

"I guess, senor that the bikers will have to deal with all Mexico police and answer for the death of their amigos." The old man answered. He rubbed his chin looking at the ground then smiled as he looked up at Ray.

"I believe, senor that this is a brilliant idea but what about these two police officers? Where do they fit in?" He was stunned by what Ray told him next.

"We cannot allow them to go away free. They will have to be killed as well." Ray watched the old man to see his reaction.

"Oh my senor. I cannot kill anyone." The old man stated nearly crying at the idea of him killing someone.

"that's alright you do not have to kill anyone. I will do the deed." Ray stated as he turned to face the two officers standing by the Lieutenant's jeep. Then telling the old man what must take place he went on.

"We will have to get them to load the jeep with the gun on it with the dead bodies of his mates. Then they must drive ahead of us to the place where we must go then I will take care of them. I want you to come with me to the place where we must go to direct us to the place. When we reach the place I will make sure there is no more problem with the police."

The old man stood where he was shaking ut attentive to what Ray was saying to him. It meant his life and the lives of his family. Spewing off in Mexican the guards put their tired hands down then started picking up the dead bodies of the fallen officers carrying them to the jeep with the heavy gun. While they were doing this Ray climbed into the jeep with the gun taking out the firing pin. If these cops had it in their mind to turn the tables by driving ahead then occupying the gun they could easily turn it against Ray and the old man. This was their need to make sure everything turned out the way it should. Once the jeep was loaded Ray motioned to the two police officers to get in and drive ahead to where they had to go. The old man did not like the police alone together so he approached Ray.

"I will take one of the pistols senor and go with the first car. You follow with the other one. This way they will not cause us any trouble."

"Good idea." Ray said as he nodded in agreement. With a pistol on them they were not foolish enough to try to do something crazy and die in their efforts. So climbing into the first jeep the old man told the officer to drive as Ray followed suit with the other officer driving the second jeep. They drove for a few hours before told to pull over to a cliff where Ray took control of the jeeps driving them to the edge. Jammed into the second seat were two officers and the Lieutenant which were stripped down naked then really jammed into the back seat. The last two officers were crying as they knew they were not getting out of this mess. Ray had them both sit in the front seat and walking up close to them he shot them twice in the back of the head. They still had the other jeep to get back to the gas station then Ray would leave for good.

They took a look off the cliff which showed a vast land of sand and some grassy spots but they also saw bikers heading their way so they had to move fast to get out of the area so heading back to the little gas station another surprise awaited them as they neared it was obvious Texas Rangers working with the Mexican police were inside the house questioning the family about Ray. Ray took the opportunity to slip the jeep off roading until he was parked about a half mile from the house leaving the jeep as both he and the old man walked slowly towards the house hoping they would not be noticed. The old man returned to the house going in to see what was transpiring. These Rangers were questioning the girls with the use of a translator which was not going too well. So the old man appeared listening to the questions as the head Ranger looked up at the old man speaking English to him.

"Can you understand me?"

"Si senor, what would you like to know?"

"I was asking your family if they had seen this person?" Holding a photo of Ray while in full uniform, it did not even look like him. The old man took the picture shaking his head no,

"No senor. No such man has come by here? Is there a danger with this man?"

"This man is very dangerous. He has killed plenty of people and we know he is somewhere here in Mexico. We are Texas Rangers and we are working with the Mexican police to try and apprehend this fellow. We need your support in trying to find him." Looking at the old man as he shook his head at the Ranger telling him.

"I do not know what you want from me senor? I have not seen such a man." The old man stood there watching the Rangers as they looked around not moving from where they sat thinking they were wasting their time.

"Okay then, if you see such a man please contact the police because he is a dangerous killer who may cause you harm if you try to help him." Passing the old man his business card he nudged at the old man to take it.

"Do you have a phone here?" The Ranger asked.

"No senor there is no phone here." Frustrated the Rangers left the house going straight down the road where the old man and Ray had come from. No doubt they would run into the bikers who would be rejoicing over finding the dead cops but more important the sub-machine gun perched on the jeep waiting for them to just take it. As the Rangers drove on they did run into the bikers who turned the sub-machine gun on them but they could not get it to fire. They had other guns with them which they used to open fire on the Rangers killing all of them but two bikers were killed in the gun battle that had ensued.

Ray made it to the back of the house when the Rangers left. Going inside the old man related to him what the Rangers had said about Ray.

"I figured this was a bad spot to rest up on so I believe I should leave and get to somewhere else where the cops will not be looking for me. I really want to thank you and your family for looking out for me and if I could repay you I am certainly in your debt. Grabbing a half bottle of tequila Ray returned to the jeep waiting for him.

He was blessed in the fact he had made some good friends here with this family. Going to the jeep Ray could see the bikers on their way to the small gas station but there were too many of them as a group of about fifty road up to the gas pumps filling their bikes. Ray stood there watching incase something bad turned out for the family. What could he do? He had the pistols from the Mexican police, each one carrying seven rounds four clips from each of them plus the additional clips added up to one hundred twelve rounds. Taking into affect of missed rounds he would be a sitting duck for these bikers to have their way with him. If somehow he could get to the jeep with the sub-machine gun, put the firing pin in that would change the odds of Ray coming out alive, saving the family and then he could move on. Ray really wanted to help so coming out from behind the garage, he slipped under a bush which hid his body from anyone coming into the backyard. What now? Seeing a group of bikers standing around the jeep Ray counted fourteen. If he fired his guns killing them the rest would bot outside to finish Ray before he could put the firing pin back in. Suddenly the bikers were called inside giving Ray a break to run to the jeep. He did and taking the gun off the stirrup which held it in place he returned to the backyard holding the sub-machine gun which was not too light. It weighed around fifty pounds itself but it had a complete chain of rounds in it. Sitting under the bush he was under earlier, Ray slipped the firing pin back into place. Could he hold the gun while it fired fifty rounds a minute? It would sap him of any strength he had but he needed to take the chance to save his friends. Watching with eagerness he wondered why the other bikers were called into the house. His mind told him the girls were in trouble and he knew if the old man tried to intervene he would end up dead. What about those darling little boys who were younger than ten years old. These bikers would not care as long as they could perform some lurid act with them fucking up their lives completely. No sitting here was not helping, Ray had to act and be at it fast if he were to be a saviour to this family. Checking the pistols under his belt, he felt his pockets to make sure the other clips were still there when he stood up holding the sub-machine gun in a menacing way. Creaping up to the back door he listened for anything that sounded out of the normality of the life of the family.

"That's it bitch, suck me dry." These pigs were having sex with the kids so reaching down for a stone Ray whipped it through a back window catching the attention of some of the bikers who came to investigate. As soon as they showed their faces Ray opened fire killing them where they stood. He had to make sure he did not waste any shots as it was vital to take as many don with the sub-machine gun as he could. Scampering feet told him they were coming out of the front to face the problem in the back so Ray squatted down not showing himself as twenty or thirty bikers with guns in their hands searched the backyard to see who threw the rock. Ray watched for his cue to open fire again. Standing up he braced his feet as the gun fired relentless at the bikers cutting some of them in two. Again voices were yelling out as Ray emptied the chamber on where he heard the voices. It had proved successful as Ray threw the sub-machine gun to the ground hauling out two pistols to fire at the remaining bikers. A few of them jumped on their bikes to get the hell out of there until another time but they were easy targets for Ray who either shot them in the back or the back of the head. He cared little about the bitches with the bikers because without the bikers to back them up they were useless. Sliding up against the house Ray cautiously moved towards the front where he saw the head biker giving orders. Taking careful aim Ray put his lights out for good. The other bikers scurried around when they commander bit the dust like rats in a fire. Not knowing what to do some of the bikers threw their weapons to the ground in hopes they could surrender to the threat upon them. Ray on the other hand showed no mercy. He emptied three guns killing them all then turning back towards the house he saw the bitches coming out as if nothing took place so slipping new clips into the guns he opened fire on them as well. Dead bodies lay around the house so when Ray walked into the house he saw one of the girls had been sodomized by a biker. The old man tried to come to her rescue but his throat had been slit from ear to ear. What a fucking waste! All this old man wanted was to enjoy living a life with his family but the disruption would never be forgotten by any of them and especially Ray who now was ready to kill as many bikers as he could.

CHAPTER XI

Ray had taken the jeep from the front where the sub-machine gun had been stationed driving further away from the house but not on the roads as he knew there was an army out looking for him. His survival meant everything to him right now to get the job done. Ray did not fear death, sometimes he prayed for it to come to him but knew if such an action took place he would never have the delight of eradicating this bike group from the face of the earth. Before leaving the house Ray stayed the night to bury his friend with the family looking on. He ate good taking a few sandwiches with him for the trip ahead. The sun was shining and the weather forecast said one hundred ten in the shade. Ray did not mind actually he liked it better than torrential rains that came this time of year. Small homes littered the desert he traveled yet it was not enough for Ray who had to keep moving on until there were warning signs of bikers in the area. Checking his gas gauge he needed some fuel if he were to carry on and just ahead were lights that lit up the night sky telling Ray a town was on the horizon. Wanting ever to go down there enjoy a few drinks and talk with someone intelligent was on Ray's mind but he could not afford the opportunity to get nabbed right now. Sitting on a hill overlooking the town Ray saw plenty of people enjoying the fine night eating, dancing and laughing. How Ray missed doing this with the woman of his dreams. Tears welled in his eyes when he thought of Clair, his woman, his wife. The many things they would be doing raising their son was the life he wanted ever so much but now that was all gone. As he thought of her he began to realize he must be going crazy because to take human life was nothing to him anymore. He thought for a moment the people he had killed. Most were bikers but there were quite a few locals who he had put don as well. What about the beginning when he had the bomb on the plane? How many innocent people had to die so he could move on with his plan. Too bad he used all the rounds from the sub-machine gun. He surely could use it now that he was at the edge of his dream. He knew he would be joining Clair soon but she was probably in heaven and he knew he wasn't going there.

Hikers came upon the jeep without Ray knowing they were there. Checking out the jeep while Ray was having a shit close by he watched them when he glanced up seeing two men check out the jeep. As he walked out of the small stand of trees he asked.

"Can I help you?" They were startled not knowing someone was with the jeep.

"Oh hello amigo. Is this your vehicle?" They were two older guys but slim built with the look of being peasants.

"What if I am?" Ray answered defensively.

"Well senor the police are looking for such a vehicle down in the town. If I drove a vehicle they were looking for I would not drive it down there."

"Is that so?" Ray said as he walked closer to the two men.

"Si senor. The police in this town," one of them said as he pointed straight to the town below them, " well they like to shoot people. I would hate to see you get shot senor for driving this vehicle into town."

"Well thanks for the warning. What's your name?"

"I am Manuel senor and this here is my friend Miguel."

"So are you from this town?"

"Oh no senor. We are from Cancun but we are on a trip hoping to get into America."

"Then how do you know about this town Manuel?"

"Well senor I have heard rumors for many years about this town. The police are known across Mexico about how ruthless they can be especially to strangers senor."

"What about the bikers Manuel? The Unholy Ones do they go there?"

"Oh no senor. The police hate the bikers so the bikers stay away from this town."

"Is there someplace I can get gas not going into this town?"

"Sure." He answered pointing off to his left. " If you continue on down there about ten miles you will come across a cantina where they sell gas as well."

"Can you come with me Manuel and show me where it is. I will pay you."

"I am not going that way senor. I am going to America."

"What if you help me out this one time and I give you the jeep as payment. Then you can ride across the desert to America. It will help you quite abit not having to walk Mauel."

"But what will you use to travel senor?"

"Well I am looking at renting a room from someone close by then stay down here for a little time."

"My aunt has a house which she rents room senor. Maybe if I show you, you will not need the jeep anymore."

"Sounds good to me. Does she live very far away?"

"No senor. She has a house not too far away but it is watched by the police incase some young senorita stays there. They like the young seoritas."

Smiling Ray knew exactly what he meant. These police took young girls and made them work the brothels so they could get a good return and if they ever wanted a blow job they knew where to go get one for free. Dirty fucking world we live in Ray thought to himself. Something had to be done.

"Okay show me where she lives." Ray said as he climbed into the jeep starting it up as Manuel and Miguel climbed in for the ride.

As they drove along Ray mentioned to Manuel.

"Why do you want to go to America?"

"Because senor it is a land where I can make a lot of money for myself and send back here to my family with hopes of them joining me." Ray started to laugh.

"I don't know who has been telling you this bullshit but believe me Manuel you are better off here in Mexico. You can work for me and I will pay you."

"Work for you senor? What must I do?" Manuel asked confused,

"Well while I am at your aunt's you can tell me if any strangers come to town and especially if any bikers show up. I will give you a couple hundred American to let me know this information."

Manuel smiled, then burst into enjoyment as he exclaimed, " Yii carumba. You would give me two hundred of your American dollars?"

"That's right Manuel and if you do a good job then maybe I would give you a bonus." Here Ray was laying down the track work to have his day with the Unholy Ones. Who else could he trust? He knew no one else in Mexico. What was a couple hundred dollars compared to doing what he wanted done? Manuel stuck his hand out to Ray with Ray grabbing hold as they shook hands making the deal solid.

Within twenty minutes more they drove along the highway away from main roads so as not to be sighted by some law enforcement agency on the lookout for Ray. With the next rise came a valley before them which Manuel pointed to a big sandstone hacienda which was where his aunt resided. There were mango trees sitting in the front yard laden with fruit and people sitting in shaded areas to keep out of the hot sun. Most of the people there were older residents who may have had rooms in the hacienda which would be a good sense of income for the aunt of Manuel. She would probably have workers looking after the upkeep of the place so why would she not hire her nephew giving him some ready cash and a place to live? This really intrigued Ray as he looked down at the acreage sitting before him wondering if these people really found their Eden enjoying life each day not worrying about tomorrow.

Driving up into the driveway of his aunt's Manual jumped out of the jeep to run into the hacienda to get his aunt bring her out to introduce Ray to her. She was a large woman which came from drinking the tequila and eating rich foods. There were no wrinkles on her tanned face as she came out of to meet this wonderful man who was going to hire her nephew.

"Hello." Ray started as he got out of the jeep. It was nice to stretch his legs from such a long trip.

"Bueno dias senor." She answered as she approached the jeep holding her hand out to shake Ray's hand.

"I understand," she began with a thick Mexican accent, " you wish to rent a room with me. I offer three meals a day but usually we have two, one in the morning the other in the cool of the evening. I offer this for 1500 pesos, a month senor."

"I like that price." Taking out eight hundred American Ray handed her the money. It paid for two months but he figured he better give it to her while he had ready cash in his pocket. Not that he would spend it because he would not venture off far from the hacienda until he got his bearings down. Manuel helped Ray carry in his bag which Ray kept an eye on as they entered the establishment as his aunt showed him the room he was entitled to. Four rooms stood out as soon as he entered the hacienda. A large room where some older women sat which must have been the living-room, Ray surmised, then off to the left was the scent of things cooking so Ray peeked into the kitchen where he saw two large stone kilns with pots boiling with the days meals for her guests. At a wooden table a woman was busy rolling dough which told Ray she was making bread for everyone. Then on the left of these rooms stood a big bathroom with a shower and bath tub along with the toilet. Ray needed to know where that was because in the still of the night he may have a hankering to use the bathroom and what an upset it would be not to know where it may be. Next to the bathroom running upstairs was a metal staircase which was hand polished to make it glimmer. The hacienda, for the size of it was spotless as it should be if people were living in it. Ray followed the aunt and Manuel up the stairs to a small bedroom which had a window he could peer out of at the front of the house. It had a twin size bed, a small dresser with four drawers, a closet where he could hang up his ruffled shirts from being in a bag so long and it had two curtains which reached the floor if he wanted to take an afternoon siesta he could close the curtains to keep the sun out. Ray was pleased with the rooming arrangement so taking his bag out of Manuel's hand Ray lay on the bed finding it rather comfortable. The aunt and Manuel left him to his room giving Ray the privacy he needed.

It was about ten minutes in the room Ray soon realized as he emptied the bag he had some clothes in on the bed that the guns were still in the jeep. Taking the empty bag downstairs with him he left the hacienda to go out to the jeep watching Manuel behind the steering wheel trying to back it up.

"HEY?" Ray yelled at him as Manuel stopped then turning to face Ray he waited until Ray came up to the jeep.

"What are you doing Manuel?" Ray asked confused that Manuel was about to leave with the vehicle.

"I am going to town to pick up some groceries for my aunt." Manuel explained.

"Did it not occur to you to ask me if you could use the jeep? There are some items in it I must take to my room." Ray told him as he opened the driver's door then reaching down to the small pocket on the door he pulled out a glock, fully loaded. Then reaching between the seats Ray pulled out another one in the same shape.

"Don't drive away yet." Ray mentioned as he went to the back of the jeep rummaging through some other less important baggage then hauled out two more guns with extra clips. Putting them in the bag he started to walk back towards the hacienda to his room. Manuel spoke out then.

"It is alright to leave now senor?"

"Yeah go ahead." Ray told him as he walked away waving to Manuel to go do his thing. What if Manuel had found the guns and sold them to someone in the town? What sort of protection would Ray then have? He was just glad he caught Manuel when he did to get his property. If any soldiers or American cops came here looking for him he wanted to be prepared but he felt this was the place to give him solace before he made his move on the bikers.

While in town Manuel went to the local bar after he fulfilled the list his aunt had given him. He still had the money Ray had given him in

American dollars so why not spend a little at the local strip joint. The place was full of bikers. Some watched him come in buying a cold beer but paying with the money Ray had given him. It seemed odd to them that this spic had so much cash on his person when everyone else carried pesos, so they questioned him.

"Hey amigo, come here for a minute." A big, burly Mexican biker called out to Manuel.

"Yes amigo?" Manuel answered as he carried his precious beer with him. Coming to a table where it was packed by bikers smiling up at Manuel they reached to another table just behind them to haul a chair so he could sit down. As Manuel sat down he took a small sip of his beer then looking at the bikers sitting all around him he smiled at them asking,

"How can I be of service to you senor?"

"We just find it funny you have American money and so much of it. How did you get so much money?" The bikers asked as they stared at Manuel.

"Well I met a gringo on my way to America and he wants me to work for him senor. He gave me the money to work for him senor."

"A gringo eh? What did he look like?"

"Well he is much older than me senor. He has gray hair mixed with some black hair. He is about six feet tall and he has plenty of guns senor."

"Is that so? Do you know where he is staying?" They asked as Manuel finished his beer. Then taking his glass they called over the bar girl.

"Hey baby fill this up for our friend." Trying to make him a friend he could trust them then maybe let them know if it were the crazy cop everyone was looking for

"What's your name?" One biker spoke out.

"I am called Manuel senor."

"So tell me Manuel. What kind of work do you do for him?" they wanted to know everything especially if it were the one they were looking for.

"He wishes me to be a lookout for him senor. When strange people show up he wishes to know or even as you as bikers come close he wishes to know."

"Is that so? Do you happen to know his name?" Manuel thought for a moment as he took another large swallow of beer.

"I did not think to ask him senor. I shall have to ask him." Manuel answered innocently.

"Yeah that would be good to know. When you go back find out for us what his name is so we can see if he is a friend of ours. When will you be back here Manuel?"

"I came to get some groceries for my aunt but maybe tomorrow in the afternoon when everyone will be inside or in the shade. It will be very hot tomorrow afternoon." Manuel stated.

"Good. Come back here and tell us his name."

"Si senor." Manuel said as he drank the last of his beer then got up to leave the bar heading back to his aunt's hacienda. It was late afternoon when Manuel made it back to the hacienda. His aunt was waiting for certain spices to be added to the evening meal so she was not too pleased her nephew took so long getting her groceries and coming home so late.

"What took you so long? I need some of those spices for supper. EYII Carumba! I should have walked to town myself at least the spices would go in at a proper time." Grabbing the bag of spices out of Manuel's hand she headed straight to the kitchen to taste test the food then add what was needed. Ray came downstairs because of all the yelling seeing Manuel under the pressures of drinking. Smiling he walked up to Manuel asking him some pertinent questions about his trip.

"So Manuel any good news with your trip?"

"I did not see any strangers senor even when I went to the bar." Taking a moment to think of the question the bikers asked Manuel went ahead with it. " Can I get your name senor?"

"Why do you need my name Manuel?" Ray asked as he moved to the shade tree sitting down beside it. His eyes never left Manuel as he thought about the reward the Mexican police would no doubt post. Was this the reason he wanted to know?

"Just in case something were to happen senor when you go to town, then I will know who to help." Manuel said. It did not make much sense to Ray for Manuel's explanation but this was Manuel he was talking to not some world known scholar.

"I see. Well I do not plan on going to town for a little while so you won't have to worry about me. I think when the time is right for me to tell you then you will find out but as it is right now my friend there is no need to know my true identity. I think you should go lay down before you fall down." Ray told him watching the disappointment on Manuel's face. Something was up with this guy so now Ray had to be extra cautious until he found out what was going on.

Ray walked into the house going straight for the bathroom to clean up for supper. His stomach was growling which let him know the spices which filled the air meant supper was nearly ready. Finally a home cooked meal to fill him. How long did he yearn for this moment with fresh baked pita bread to help clean his plate with the delights that Manuel's aunt created. Still there was time for Ray to wait so he decided to wait in the living room. There was another elderly couple waiting as well and they had been with the aunt for nearly ten years now. Why not? This was a little slice of heaven for the tenants who had the opportunity to stay here.

Soon a chime rang which meant supper was ready to be served. The elderly couple had their spot where they sat at each meal so Ray decided to wait until his seat was given him from the aunt. She came into the dining hall with two other women all carrying the provisions for the meal. Plates of fresh baked bread were placed on the dining room table as Manuel and Miguel picked a seat to place themselves at the table. Ray had the rare opportunity to sit right beside the aunt as she motioned for him to sit beside her. Coming over to the table, Ray sat down taking the cloth napkin placing it on his lap, he waited until the plates were passed his way but the aunt decided to serve him giving him a large helping of the chili con carne she prepared for the meal. Taking four slices of the hot bread she placed them just before Ray's plate so he would have easy access to them. The meal was quiet with no one talking and the only noise was the slurping and chewing of the delightful meal. Ray took his time making sure he was not the first to finish but he certainly wanted a second helping. Cold vanilla ice cream was the dessert of choice to off-set the hot chili they ate. It was a welcome relief from the hot spices permeating their palates. After the meal Ray retired to his room to lie on his bed looking out the window from there at the golden sunset which told him tomorrow would be another hot day. Ray's thoughts went back to Manuel, what was he up too? There had to be a reasonable reason why he wanted Ray's name. ray knew he had to keep an eye on him especially when he went to town.

The next morning Ray confronted Manuel once again to find out what was happening.

"Manuel are you going into town today?"

"I can if you wish me to senor."

"Yeah I wouldn't mind going in myself and check things out. Would you come with me?"

"Why yes senor. It is better than lying around here all day." Miguel came over to them hoping he could join them when they went to town but Ray did not need Miguel around, he would probably get in the way anyways.

"When would you like to go senor?" Manuel asked smiling up at Ray.

"A little later." Ray said as he walked back into the hacienda to speak with the aunt.

"I am going to town today do you need anything?" Ray asked.

"No senor I got what I needed yesterday with my nephew, but thank you for asking." Turning Ray walked back out in the yard calling Manuel to him.

"Manuel get ready we should leave in about a half hour." Manuel came running up to the jeep looking forward to taking Ray into the town to see if he could get a reward from the bikers if he were the one they were looking for.

Going back inside the house Ray headed straight to his room taking two stairs at a time but he reached the top he was short of breath. He realized he was getting older as his youth escaped him. Going into his room he went straight to the closet where he had his weapons. Taking one of the pistols he also brought along an extra clip in case he ran into any trouble along the way. Grabbing a shirt out of the closet he put it on over his tee shirt to look representable in case he met anyone of importance or a nice looking senorita he would try to bed. Finally ready to leave Ray made his way downstairs a little slower taking his time as he needed all the strength he had so if he were confronted then he would have the strength to put up a fight.

Outside Manuel was sitting in the jeep waiting for Ray so they could go to town. Ray wanted a smoke before he left so taking the pack of smokes which were in his shirt pocket, he took one out then slapped his pockets to see which one housed his lighter. Finding it in his right pants pocket he took it out lighting his smoke then returning the lighter to his right hand pants pocket. Taking a long haul felt good for him as he exhaled his smoke letting the gray-blue acrid smoke leave his body. Ray cared little for second-hand smoke and the dangers it did to his neighbors. After getting three quarters of the cigarette smoked he flicked the butt into the driveway, climbed onto the jeep then started the engine. Looking over at Manuel he was just sitting there smiling which made Ray feel he was being set-up so he had to be on the watch for any hidden snares. It took them over an hour to reach the main square of the town so splitting up Ray wanted Manuel to play his hand so he let him go on his own meeting up a little later.

"Manuel it's eleven thirty so say we meet up here in about an hour." Ray stated.

"That is fine senor." Manuel answered then went his way. Ray stood where he was watching Manuel until he took the next corner. Walking around the different shops Ray was really pleased with the sidewalk shops of fresh vegetables and fruits. Picking out a large, juicy peach, he paid for it then bit into it sending juice down his face but the flavor was full and very delicious. Ray kept looking at his watch to see what time it was so he could meet up with Manuel to find out some more bit of news of him finding out anything which would help his situation. The sun was starting to get straight up in the sky as the temperature was 110 in the shade. Beads of sweat ran down Ray's face from his forehead which he did not mind as he was enjoying a glass of tequila. Ray had found out that drinking a cold beer made it worse but the tequila made from the agave plant, the best tequila did not have much affect when he drank it in the heat of the day. Looking up he saw Manuel heading his way and he was interested in what Manuel had found out. Coming to his side Ray bought Manuel a glass of tequila as they talked.

"Find anything interesting?" Ray asked as Manuel made himself comfortable at the table.

"Senor there is talk of a few dangerous people, senor, looking for you. They were here in the marketplace this morning senor." Taking a sip of his drink he went on. " Maybe you would like senor, I should help you find these men?"

Ray turned to him looking him straight in the eyes as he asked.

"You know where these people are staying? Do you know how many?"

Ray stopped short as he mentioned, " hold on Manuel. Maybe if you told me what room they were in, I could surprise them."

"Ok senor. They are on the first right at the top of the stairs." Manuel stated. Ray knew now Manuel was playing him or how else would he know this vital information?

"What's your brother's name?" Ray asked trying to squeeze as much information out of Manuel before the little greaser knew what was going on.

"His name is Fredo."

"Will you show me your brother's home?"

"Oh yes senor." Manuel seemed rather pleased Ray would be going to his brother's home to meet

these dangerous people.

"Ok when we get there I want you to point out the house for me." Manuel said nothing but nodded in agreement.

"Okay Manuel I want you to go back to the jeep and wait for me. I will go see who these dangerous people are and handle the situation."

"Okay senor."

Manuel was already on his way back to the jeep as Ray made his move. Going to the stairs Ray walked softly as one squeak from the stairs could cost him his life. Reaching the top of the stairs Ray waited a moment then tightly squeezing the handle of the door he turned it softly. A small click told him the door was open, so with extra care Ray opened the door so very carefully as he did not want to catch a bullet. Finding the room empty, Ray eased the grip he had on the gun. Turning to leave ray was not expecting a full punch on the jaw from Wally "wagon hillside," Price who had all his strength in the punch sending Ray to the floor out cold. Ray was unconscious not feeling the bikers taking him out of the room to their bikes down on the street below. Starting up their bikes they headed out of town out into the desert regions where no one really ventured, not even the cops because it was so damn hot. They had a surprise for the renegade cop who wanted to see all bikers destroyed. This cop had killed a lot of the bikers who were milestones with the Unholy Ones so he had to pay dearly for the errors he committed against them.

Taking his legs they tied them to two different bikes then did the same to his arms being tied to two different bikes. Waking Ray up to get him completely conscious they began revving their engines as Wally looked at him telling him, " this one is for Sheryl."

Ray remembered her words, " I have friends all over the world. I'll get the last laugh." Wondering what these fucker's were going to do, he got his painful answer without raising a question. Four bikers driving in four directions from Ray tore his legs and arms from his body. All that was left was a bouncing, throbbing mass in the middle of the desert.

Manuel was there to witness the carnage the bikers did. He was horrified as he looked at the smiles and cheering the bikers made. Good thing Manuel made them his friends as they were ruthless in their ways. So going to them as they had made camp where the execution was made.

"Here comes our friend Manuel. How ya doing man?" They asked as Manuel walked closer to the lion's den.

"Hey Manuel come over here." Destroyer called out to Manuel. Destroyer was the Vice President of the Unholy Ones. As Manuel got closer Destroyer asked him, " I suppose you want your reward right now." Manuel nodded in agreement with him as Destroyer got up to take a short walk with him.

"Well we promised you a fine reward for turning your friend over to us." Destroyer told Manuel as he had his arm around his shoulders then went on to tell Manuel what his reward would be.

"I am sorry Manuel but you were a traitor to your friend so we cannot trust you. You have to die." Manuel's cries fell upon the desert sands then they buried him under a foot of the sand. Mounting their bikes they headed back to the States.

The End